THE SILVER BRUMBY

As a distinguished writer for children about Australian history and the environment since 1942, Elyne Mitchell still writes today at 86.

Elyne published her first book in 1942, and her first children's novel, *The Silver Brumby*, appeared in 1958. With this book, Elyne began a series of highly successful novels for children which introduced them to the wild brumbies of Australia and the natural beauty of the Australian landscape. In 1993 a feature film of *The Silver Brumby* was released, and an animated TV series of the book was produced in 1995–96 and sold all over the world. During the 1980s Elyne also wrote non-fiction, including autobiographical works about her family, the Chauvels, and her years at Towong Hill, where she has lived since 1936.

In 1990 Elyne received the Order of Australia Medal, and in 1993 was awarded an honorary Doctor of Letters from Charles Sturt University for literature. She still lives on the family property on the Victorian and New South Wales border, rides her own horse whenever she can and swims in the lagoon.

Throughout her life, Elyne has written about her love of the land. From her first compost heap in 1945 to her annual planting of six hundred eucalyptus trees and native shrubs in Towong Hill, Elyne's commitment to the environment is a legacy many readers take from her work.

This book was written for Indi
who loves horses

Collins Modern Classics

The Silver Brumby

by

Elyne Mitchell

Illustrated by
Ralph Thompson

Collins
An imprint of HarperCollinsPublishers

First published in Great Britain by Hutchinson & Co. Ltd 1958
First published by Collins 1992
First published as a Collins Modern Classic 1999

1 3 5 7 9 10 8 6 4 2

Collins Modern Classics is an imprint of HarperCollins*Publishers* Ltd,
77-85 Fulham Palace Road, Hammersmith, London W6 8JB

The HarperCollins website address is
www.**fire**and**water**.com

ISBN 0 00 675470-8

Printed and bound in Great Britain by
Caledonian International Book Manufacturing Ltd,
Glasgow, G64

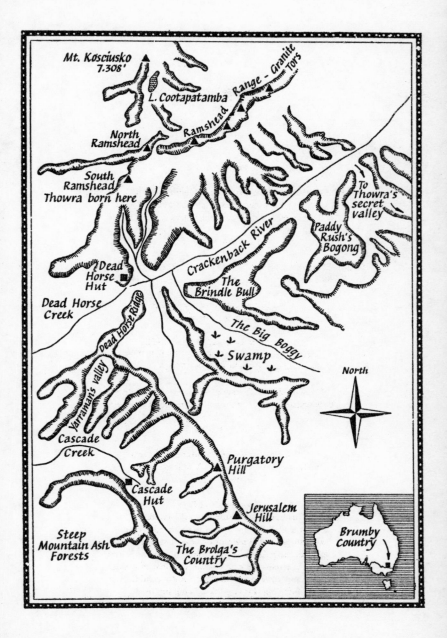

Mt. Kosciusko
7.308'

L. Cootapatamba

Ramshead Range – Granite Tors

North Ramshead

South Ramshead
Thowra born here

To Thowra's secret valley

Crackenback River

Paddy Rush's Bogong

Dead Horse Hut

The Brindle Bull

Dead Horse Creek

Dead Horse Ridge

The Big Boggy

Swamp

North

Yarraman's valley

Cascade Creek

Purgatory Hill

Cascade Hut

Jerusalem Hill

Steep Mountain Ash Forests

The Brolga's Country

Brumby Country

CONTENTS

Chapter One

BORN IN THE WILD WIND

ONCE THERE WAS a dark, stormy night in spring, when, deep down in their holes, the wombats knew not to come out, when the possums stayed quiet in their hollow limbs, when the great black flying phallangers that live in the mountain forests never stirred. On this night, Bel Bel, the cream brumby mare, gave birth to a colt foal, pale like herself, or paler, in that wild, black storm.

Bel Bel had chosen the birthplace of the foal wisely. He was on springy snowgrass under a great overhang of granite that sheltered them from the driving rain. There he lay, only a pale bundle in the black dark, while Bel Bel licked him clean and nuzzled him. The wind roared and howled through the granite tors above in the Ramshead Range, where the snow still lay, but there was no single sound of animal or bird except the mournful howl of a dingo –

once, twice, it rang out and its echo answered, weird and wild.

Bel Bel lifted her head at the sound, and her nostrils dilated. From the shadowy mass between her forefeet came a faint nickering cry and she nuzzled him again. She was very alone with her newborn foal, and far from her own herd, but that was how she had felt it must be. Perhaps because of her colour, so much more difficult to hide than bay, or brown, black, or grey or chestnut, she had always led a hunted life, and when a foal was going to be born she was very nervous and hid herself far away. Of the three foals she had had, this was the only one creamy, like herself.

Bel Bel felt a surge of pride, but the pride was followed by fear. Her son would be hunted as she was and as her own cream mother had been before her – hunted by man, since they were so strange-looking in the wild herds. And this colt would have another enemy too, every stallion would be doubly against him because of his colour.

The wind roared and the rain was cold, so cold, as if it would turn to snow. Even with the shelter of the rock, the storm was beating down on them, the moving darkness was becoming a thing of terror. The howl of the dingo came again. Bel Bel nosed the tiny colt to get up.

He heaved up his head, stuck his long forelegs out in front of him, and gave a little snort of fear. Bel Bel pushed him up till he stood, his feet far apart, long legs trembling; then she nosed him, wobbling, bending, step by step to the sandy mouth of a cave, and there, just out of the rain, she let him tumble down again.

Soon it would be time to make him drink, but for the moment, out of the wild storm, he could rest. Dawn must come soon, and in this storm there would be no men abroad to see a cream brumby mare lead her newborn foal through the snowgums to where there would be grass for her to eat and longed-for water to drink. Bel Bel really knew that there would be very few men in the mountains till all the snow had gone and they came driving their herds of red-and-white cattle, but the fear of Man was never far from her thoughts.

Dawn came very slowly, showing first the dark outline of the cave mouth against a faintly lighter sky, then, on the hillside below them, reaching long fingers of forest right up to the rocks, the wind-tormented heads of snowgums, driven and lashing as though they must tear themselves up by the roots. The rain had stopped.

Great massing clouds kept racing up over the mountains, but, as the light grew strong, the sky began to look as if it was being torn in shreds by the wind. Flying streamers of rain-washed blue sky appeared and Bel Bel, feeling very hungry herself, decided it was time the foal should drink and that the day would be fair enough for a newborn colt to go with his mother to some better pastures.

"I will call you Thowra," she said, waking him with her nose, "because that means wind. In wind were you born, and fleet as the wind must you be if you will live."

On that first day, while the storm blew itself out, Bel Bel did not take Thowra far, only down through the snowgums to a long glade that led to a heather-banked creek where she could drink. That night they went back to the opening of the cave and the foal slept on the dry sand curled up against his mother's flank.

The next day she decided to take him farther, to a wide, open field in the snowgum forest, where the grass grew very sweetly, even as early in the spring as this, and where the creek ran shallow over a sand and mica bottom.

The storm had died in the night and there was warm spring sunshine. Bel Bel noticed with pride how the foal trotted more strongly by her side. She did not hurry him, often stopping to graze as they moved under the snowgums or in the long glades. She never left the shelter of the trees without first pausing and looking carefully into the open country ahead. Thus it was through a curtain of the leathery snowgum leaves that she looked out on to the wide, sunny field, and saw a bay brumby grazing in the distance by the creek.

Bel Bel became completely still, watching: then she recognized the bay as a mare of her own herd, Mirri, who had been caught by a stockman as a yearling, and managed to get free. Mirri, for this reason, was very nervous of men, and she and Bel Bel had often run together, away from the herd, when they thought the others were too close to the stockmen's huts.

Now Bel Bel made out a dark shape on the ground near Mirri and knew that the bay mare, too, had her foal. Unafraid, she led Thowra out to join them.

When Mirri saw them coming she gave a whinny of greeting, and Bel Bel arched her neck a little and stepped

proudly beside her creamy son, thinking how his mane and
tail were silver and would someday look like spray from a
waterfall as he galloped.

Mirri was pleased to see her.

"Well met, Bel Bel," she said, "and what a fine foal you
have — creamy too! I must stir my sleepy-head to show him
off!" And she nosed the bright bay at her feet.

The bay raised his head sleepily, but, seeing strangers, he
became wide awake and struggled to his feet.

"A fine intelligent head," Bel Bel said. "What do you
call him?"

"Storm," Mirri answered. "He was born in the worst of
the weather, two nights ago. And yours?"

"Thowra, for the wind. He was born then too. They will
be great mates for a year or so," and both mothers nodded
wisely, for was it not the way of the wild horses that the
young colts should run together, after they left their dams,
until they had reached the age and strength to fight for a
mare or two of their own and start their own herd.

Storm and Thowra sniffed at each other curiously and
then both turned back to their mothers for a drink.

Sunny spring days came, day after day, and the grass grew
fresh, and green, and sweet. The two mares stayed in
Snowgrass Plain, eating, basking in the sun, drinking the
cold, clear water, growing strong and sleek after the hard
winter, and giving their foals plenty of milk. The foals grew
strong, too, and romped and galloped, and rolled in the sun.

Soon they learned to recognize the great wedge-tail
eagles floating in the blue arch of sky above them, knew the

call of kurrawongs, and were unafraid of the friendly grey kangaroos or little brown wallabies.

The two foals were equal in strength and size, and when they were able to follow their mothers for quite a long distance, Bel Bel and Mirri, who had become restless to rejoin the herd, started moving off to the south.

For an hour or so they travelled across the ridge tops, in the fringe of the snowgums, and by mid-morning they came out on an immense open hillside, which was half of a great basin in the hills. Bel Bel and Mirri checked the foals at the edge of the tree line.

"Never run out into clear country without first taking a very good look," they warned.

The foals could see nothing except steep snowgrass and rocks dropping down, down beyond their sight, and away over opposite, a rough, timbered hillside.

"That's where we will spend some of the summer," Bel Bel said. "It is too rough for the men and their cattle, but we get a good picking there."

Neither Thowra nor Storm knew what she meant.

"Down there," said Mirri, "is the Crackenback River. A nice, cool stream to drink at on hot days, and good sandy beaches, in places, for young ones to roll on."

They moved out on to the clear hillside, but never went far from the shelter of the trees. Thowra and Storm were too pleasantly tired to want to play and soon dropped to sleep in the sunshine. Bel Bel and Mirri grazed contentedly, a little distance off. All was quiet. There was the far-off sound of the river, running full and strong with water from the melted snows, and the sound of kurrawongs, but otherwise a profound silence. Even the mares had grown sleepy, when all of a sudden there was a shrill whinny of fear from Thowra.

Bel Bel whipped round in time to see Thowra and Storm leaping up from their sleep, and there, grabbing at Thowra as he leapt, was a man. She neighed, calling her foal to come quickly, and started galloping towards them, ready to strike at the man. The foals, with long legs flailing, were racing towards her, wild with fear.

She heard Mirri scream with rage behind her. Then the man turned and ran into the trees.

The mares stopped in their headlong chase to snuff their trembling foals all over and make sure they were unhurt.

Bel Bel was all for chasing the man.

"He was no stockman, he had no rope or whip," she said.

"No," answered Mirri, "but even a man alone, walking through the mountains, sometimes has a gun. No, we will thankfully take our foals and go." She turned to Storm. "See, my son, that was a man. Never go near Man, nor his huts, nor his yards where he fences in cattle and his own tame horse. Man will hurt you and capture you; put straps of leather rope upon your head, tie you up, fence you in, beat you if you bite or kick…" She was sweating with fear as she spoke, and the two foals' trembling increased.

"And you, Thowra," said Bel Bel, "I told you you would have to be as fleet as the wind. For your creamy coat and your silver mane and tail they will hunt you, so that they may ride astride your back over your own mountains. Beware of Man!"

Still sweating with fear, the two mares led their foals away, slipping like wraiths between the trees, trotting steeply down, trotting, trotting.

After quite a long way they were getting near the head of the stream. Here the mares went more slowly, stopping to sniff the air.

"It is from this hut he must have come, but he is not back yet," Bel Bel said.

"There may be others." Mirri's nostrils were quivering.

"I can smell no fresh smoke."

"But, still, let us drop much lower down and cross the stream there, rather than follow the track near the hut."

Bel Bel rubbed one ear on a foreleg.

"The foals are very tired," she said. "We had better spend the night near water. A drink for us will make more milk for them too."

They slept that evening well below the head of the Crackenback, with the singing stream beside them, but occasionally when the north wind blew, the two mares would wrinkle their nostrils and mutter between their teeth, "Smoke!" So when the moon rose, they nosed the foals up on their tired legs and started the long climb up the Dead Horse Ridge. Once up on top, they could afford to rest again, but it took the poor foals hours to climb it, and when they found a soak of water to drink, just beyond the top, the mares let the little ones drop down on the soft ground and sleep undisturbed till daybreak.

From there on the travelling was easy, and Bel Bel and Mirri were not so anxious. They were a long way from the hut, and getting very close to the wild horses' winter and spring grazing grounds where, until the snows had all gone, they were never bothered by men.

There had been a time once, years and years ago, when four people had come whizzing down the snow-covered ridges with great wooden boards on their feet, and one of them had a lasso and had roped a bay colt; but they had been laughing, laughing – mad, in fact – for all they wanted was to cut off some of his tail to wear plaited and pinned on their coats. This was a legend among the wild horses, a tale every foal heard... but it had happened a long time ago, and Man was not expected in the Cascades until the herds of cattle came for summer grazing.

It was evening when the four of them looked down into a narrow valley off the Cascades, and saw their own herd grazing. Just then the great golden chestnut stallion, leader of the herd, raised his head and saw them and let out a shrill trumpeting cry of greeting.

The two mares neighed in reply and started trotting down the long slope, followed by their nervous foals.

Kookaburra

Chapter Two

YARRAMAN'S HERD

THOWRA AND STORM were both really frightened by the excitement of the great stallion, their father, and the curiosity of the other mares and foals.

One huge chestnut foal sniffed at Thowra and then gave him a sharp, unpleasant bite on the wither. Thowra dodged behind Bel Bel who promptly laid her ears back and chased the foal away. A small, mean-looking brown mare came prancing up and bared her teeth at Bel Bel.

"That's my foal, Bel Bel," she snarled.

"Should have thought as much," Bel Bel said. "There's nothing in your looks that a foal *could* take after, so it had to be the image of its father." But when the brown mare had moved off and left them, she said to Thowra: "Watch that foal, son. It may only be as much as a week older than you but it's much bigger, and, though its got its father's looks, it has inherited its mother's mean spirit."

"What's more," said Mirri, "Brownie will be trying to queen it over everyone just because she has produced a foal so like Yarraman." Then she called out loudly to Brownie, "What have you named your colt?"

"Arrow," came the answer.

Though the weeks that followed were peaceful for the herd, they were not really peaceful for Thowra and Storm. Arrow seemed to hold it against them that they had been born far off below the Ramshead Range, farther and higher than he had ever been. Whenever Bel Bel and Mirri moved off grazing, or the foals galloped away from their mothers, Arrow would appear slyly beside them, giving a quick bite, or kicking as he galloped past. The other foals were mostly afraid of him, too, but apt to follow his lead – when they could be bothered. Fortunately for Thowra and Storm they could not often be bothered, it was so much pleasanter to gallop and prance on the soft grass, or to splash in the ice-cold creek, watching the golden spray fly up.

Bel Bel and Mirri knew that Arrow was bossing all the foals, that he was being particularly spiteful towards Thowra and Storm. They kept an eye on any rough games, but realized that the foals must learn to take care of themselves, too.

The days, to the foals, were almost all the same. They drank the good milk from their mothers, slept in the sun, and played. They learned to stand with forelegs far apart so that they could stretch down and nibble the sweet snowgrass. They learnt other things, too. Bel Bel and Mirri taught them to recognize the track of a dingo, whose cry they heard through the darkness of the night, to tell the wombat paths through the damp bush, and the narrow trail of the Evil One, the snake, over sand; they taught them, too, to recognize the hoofmarks and scent of each member of their herd, and to tell when strange horses came close.

Several other herds of brumbies grazed in the Cascades. They saw one quite large herd one day when Bel Bel and Mirri felt they must wander and took the foals up Salt Yard Hill at the head of the huge Cascades Valley. Thowra became very excited over their tracks, and proud of himself for recognizing them as strangers. He became prouder still when Bel Bel and Mirri showed great interest in one particular set of hoofmarks, one particular scent.

"That's The Brolga," they muttered, and blew through their nostrils with excitement. "And he's got quite a big herd."

"Who's The Brolga?" the foals both asked.

"He is a young grey stallion, for he will beat Yarraman when he attains his full strength."

Thowra and Storm had learnt enough by now to know that this would be a terrific fight, and they wandered up on the grassy hill dreaming of perhaps seeing the great Brolga and his herd.

The restless mares grazed their way on to the southern-most flank of the hill and there, below, on a flat valley floor, were The Brolga and his mares and foals.

Storm started to whinny with excitement, but Mirri gave him a swift nip on the shoulder.

"Be quiet, silly fellow," she said. "They might not be pleased to see us."

Thowra was trembling.

"See," said Bel Bel, "three grey filly foals."

"Come on," Mirri nudged Storm, "we'd better get back the other way."

The sun was lovely and warm, and it was good to be up above the valley looking down on all the familiar country with its gleaming creeks that ran on down till they joined together and rushed over the rocky rapids. These rapids were the start of the huge waterfall that tumbled down, and down, and down, how far, no brumby knew.

That day there was a particularly shining look to all the snowgums, as if the sunlight was dripping off their leaves. The four looked around with satisfaction, grazed back across the face of the hill, slept for a while in the sun, and then started wandering back towards their own herd.

Bel Bel looked behind her several times, as was her usual habit, and just as evening was drawing on, she saw something which made her heart jolt inside her. Nose down to their tracks, following a long way behind, was The Brolga with several other horses – young colts and dry mares, she guessed.

"We'd better run for it, Mirri, as fast as the foals can go," she said. "Look behind!"

Mirri looked back over her shoulder and snorted quite quietly, but her ears flickered back and forth. "You two should know your way back to the herd," she said sharply to Storm. "Bel Bel and I will just plod along and keep The Brolga thinking."

"It would be better to keep together," said Bel Bel,

knowing that even in the dusk her foal would show up clearly. "Come quickly."

She led off at a hard gallop with the foals following and Mirri bringing up the rear. She knew that The Brolga and his companions would hear them as soon as they started to gallop, but there was a good chance that, despite the slow foals, their lead on The Brolga would allow them to reach their own herd before he caught up with them.

"Hurry," she called back over her shoulder. "Hurry!" And though she could hear no sound except their own hoof-beats, she caught a glimpse of galloping horses way behind.

They galloped on and on and she could hear the foals beside her blowing. Then she led them splashing through the creek and swung round some rocks and up into the narrow valley where Yarraman's herd had spent each night for some time now. There, she raised her head and let out a high-pitched neigh for help, urging the foals on.

In the gloom near the top of the valley she saw Yarraman, head up, light golden mane and tail foaming, trotting along, looking inquiringly down the valley. She called again and he and some of the herd behind him started to gallop.

From behind her she heard the wild scream of a stallion. She looked back again. The Brolga was standing at the turn into the valley, one foot raised, his head thrown up as he called.

Bel Bel whistled through her teeth. Now what was going to happen? She slowed up. The foals need not gallop so fast. The Brolga would forget all about everyone except Yarraman.

Yarraman began to gallop in earnest. He went thundering past them down the valley, golden mane and tail streaming out on the wind that was made by his own speed. The two mares stopped and turned round to watch. The Brolga was advancing up the valley, rearing and screaming. Bel Bel looked at Thowra, who was giving little whinnies of fear, his eyes and nostrils dilated.

"Oh, well, he must learn what fighting is like," she thought, "because he, too, will have to fight."

As he drew close to The Brolga, Yarraman stopped in his headlong gallop and pawed the ground, screaming. Then the two horses advanced, rearing and trumpeting until they were within striking distance of each other and could aim wicked blows with their forefeet.

Even in the half light into which, being grey, The Brolga seemed to fade, the other horses could see how much less heavy and less developed he was than Yarraman. They all knew, too, that in years of fighting, Yarraman had learnt every trick. Perhaps, they thought, he will not consider it right or worth his while to kill or maim a much younger horse, and will only punish him for following some of his herd.

The screaming was tremendous. All that could be seen were the two horses, on their hind legs, one a streak of chestnut, pale in the pale light, the other a fainter streak of grey in the gloom, sometimes locked together, biting, striking. Occasionally they broke apart, dropped to the ground and danced around to get in a good position to kick. Yarraman tried not to let The Brolga break away too often because the light, younger horse was more nimble on his feet and he had already managed to give one very savage kick.

All the watching horses were trembling and sweating with fear and excitement. Those from The Brolga's herd had drawn a little down the valley. Sometimes their neighs could be heard above the noise of the two stallions.

"Listen! They are calling the foolish one away," said Bel Bel, and added softly, "it grows dark."

Soon they could barely see the two horses.

"See! They are backing off, looking at each other," Mirri murmured. "It is too dark, and Yarraman has punished him enough."

Bel Bel could just distinguish the grey shadow of The Brolga, risen on his hind legs again, but backing down the valley. Then it was night.

Yarraman, snorting, whinnying, and tossing his fine head, a dark stain of blood on his shoulder and neck, came trotting up the valley.

Spiny Anteater or Echidna

Chapter Three

LEADING THE FOALS A DANCE

NOT LONG AFTER this, when the weather was becoming much warmer, Yarraman suddenly led his herd off, away from the Cascades towards the rough range that the mares had pointed out to the foals on the other side of the Crackenback River. When they got there was a whole new world to be discovered — not the wide valleys and spacious grassland of the Cascades, with large snowgums and sometimes candlebarks, but rough, rocky ridges and stunted trees, tiny threads of streams, and hidden pockets of snowgrass.

The foals enjoyed it. They played hide-and-seek in among the rocky tors and challenged each other to races down the steep hillsides where the stones broke away from under their hooves and went clattering down, down, even faster than they could go. Best of all were the bathing parties in the Crackenback, when the days grew really hot, and they could splash and blow bubbles in the water where it ran over the cool, brown stones and the shining mica; and then they would chase each other and roll in the sand.

The foals were two months old, and Mirri and Bel Bel had lost no opportunity of teaching them their way around the new country. None of the other mares wandered so far off on their own and, when it came to a really good game of hide-and-seek, none of the other foals knew the country as well as Thowra and Storm did.

Brownie was a lazy mare. She stayed around near Yarraman, queening it, as Mirri had guessed she would, and Arrow learnt little else than to be a nuisance – in fact, what else could Brownie teach him, Bel Bel said – but he was still the biggest and strongest foal in the herd. Several times he had given Thowra or Storm vicious bites, and once Thowra was lamed for a week by a kick on the hock.

Then, one hot, sultry day, with big thunder clouds sitting lazily along the mountain tops, Arrow was stung, it seemed, to thorough nastiness by the great March flies, and he chased Thowra, biting him unmercifully.

Thowra called Storm:

"Come on!" he said. "He won't catch us!" And away they galloped with Arrow and half the other foals after them.

"We'll lead them a dance," Thowra said to Storm, as they galloped side by side down into a steep ravine. "If we can lose Arrow, we will!"

They went crashing down, Arrow and his followers not far behind, down, down the rocky slope and then into some very thick scrub. Here, Thowra pulled up sharply on his haunches, and swung on to a tiny narrow track that led towards the head of the ravine.

They heard the other foals go thundering by straight on down, while they went trotting quietly on, making as little sound as possible. The track turned upwards, and they knew they would be quite a height above the other foals when they got out of the scrub.

Thowra led the way on to the rocky hillside again and, sure-footed as a wild goat, cantered across it upwards to the tumbled mass of rock that formed the headwall of the ravine. He and Storm had found a track through, but he was pretty certain Arrow would not know it. He looked down once and saw the other foals far below, but already starting in pursuit.

They had to let their pace drop to a walk when they reached the rocks, and for a moment it was hard to find the start of their track; then they picked their way carefully through, and round and over the great rough rocks with almost a sheer wall of rock up on one side of them and a tremendous drop on the other.

They could hear the other foals crashing and stumbling across the side of the hill, but they didn't stop or look back: they had to watch every step they took on their precipice or they might find themselves hurtling down through space to the floor of the ravine, far below. Thowra felt his coat prickling with fear, and then the sweat running on his neck and flanks. How foolish it would be to fall! But at last they were over, and there, safe on the other side, they neighed and mocked at Arrow who was still looking for a way across the headwall.

At this, Arrow became so angry that he started to climb right round over the top. Thowra and Storm could afford to rest before galloping off. Then they were off again, through very broken country of granite tors, rough scrub, and low snowgums, directly away from where the mares had been grazing. There was no grass here, and Thowra guessed that the other foals had never bothered to explore this way.

Both foals noticed how hot it had become. Thowra's cream coat was all dark with sweat. They stopped for a moment to get their breath and watched black clouds massing over the sky.

"We may be glad we know our way," Thowra said.

The others were drawing nearer, so they led them on, up a little hill. Already the grey mist was sitting on top of it.

As soon as they saw the other foals following up the hill, they went through the mist and quickly down the other side, then jumped down into a sharp-sided creek bed that cut straight across the foot of the hill. They turned east up the creek and trotted along, presently stopping for a drink.

There was no sound of pursuit, although once Thowra thought he heard a neigh.

"This creek will take us nearly all the way home," he said.

"Yes," Storm answered. "Come!"

"I'm wondering about the others."

They both looked around. Clouds had boiled up and poured right over the mountains, and it was impossible to see more than a few yards.

"It's all very well to get Arrow lost on a fine day," Thowra said, "but the weather is changing. Also," he added, "the mothers of the other foals will be wild with us, even if they do think Arrow deserves all he gets."

"That is quite true," Storm said. "Perhaps we had better go and find them."

They went back along the creek, and scrambled up on to the hillside again. Now, they could hear neighing coming from the top of the hill.

Storm threw up his head to listen:

"I expect they are wandering round in circles," he said. "Don't let's hurry; give them time to get to know what it's like being lost in a cloud."

But when they reached the top of the hill they could just make out the group of foals through the cloud, all huddled together in the shelter of some rocks.

Thowra and Storm went up to them, emerging like shadows out of the mist.

"Don't you know your way home?" Storm asked.

Arrow said nothing, but the other foals came crowding round.

"Can you lead us back even through these clouds?" they asked.

Thowra looked at them without speaking for a moment, then he turned to Arrow.

"Do you want to go home, O swift Arrow?"

Arrow nodded glumly. Just then there was a great roll of thunder, and a whip-like streak of lightning seemed to strike the rocks. Thowra took no notice.

"Are you going to behave yourself and be nicer to everyone else?" he asked Arrow.

There was no answer.

"Oh well," said Thowra, "Storm and I will go home on our own," and he moved as if to go back into the cloud and mist. More lightning blazed behind him, and he seemed to be made of silver.

The other foals crowded after them but Arrow stood quite still.

"Arrow will behave, or we will all set on him this minute," spoke up Star, a brown filly who had always wished she could go wandering with Thowra and Storm and their mothers.

"All right," Thowra and Storm both agreed. "Follow us then, closely." Their last words were almost lost in the rumble of thunder and the sudden sound of pouring rain.

Shivering with cold now as well as fear, the foals followed them as they turned and made their way down into the more sheltered creek bed. Here, the noise of the thunder was almost like something striking at them, and Thowra noticed with pleasure that Arrow was as frightened as the others.

In places the creek bed widened, and there was grass or sand over which they could canter; sometimes they walked through stones. Then the creek turned in a long northward curve that led them back towards where the herd had been. Even when they were quite close to the mares, the clouds were so heavy and black that only Thowra and Storm knew they had arrived back.

Quietly they led the foals into the herd. They could tell by the restless moving of the mares that they were worried. Brownie gave a silly-sounding neigh when she saw Arrow and started sniffing him all over.

"What have you been up to?" muttered Bel Bel as Thowra came up beside her for a drink.

"Maybe Arrow won't be such a bully for a while," Thowra answered.

"Take care – that colt may always be bigger and stronger than you," Bel Bel said.

Just then Star's mother came up.

"No good will come of you teaching your sons to be so independent," she said to Bel Bel and Mirri angrily, and then turned to Thowra. "Where have you led our foals to, today?" But Star, looking miserable, said:

"It was our fault – and Arrow's."

"That Arrow!" said the mare sourly. "He will grow into a bad horse."

"He'll be a bad enemy," said Mirri, looking with meaning at her own son and at Thowra.

Phallanger or Flying Possum

Chapter Four

BRUMBY DRIVE

ON VERY CLEAR days the wild horses could see the cattle grazing on the other side of the Crackenback River. Sometimes they might meet an odd beast down drinking, but the horses mostly kept to drinking places where the cattle never came, because where there were cattle there could be men.

One day Bel Bel and Mirri and the two foals were climbing up behind a particularly high granite tor. They were still in the trees, and out of sight themselves, when they saw a man standing upon the top of the tor, gazing over the country.

The wild horses came to a dead stop, nostrils quivering. There the man stood, a wide hat shading his eyes, a red scarf round his neck, wearing faded riding-trousers, and with a coiled whip in his hand.

"Stockman," whispered Bel Bel. "His tame horse must be somewhere, and maybe a mate or two. Our scent must be blowing straight to him."

"*He* won't smell it," said Mirri scornfully.

"His horse may, though."

Sure enough, there came the sound of neighing and stamping, and even the jingle of a bit.

"It's not very far away. We must go!" Bel Bel turned to Thowra: "Look well at the man, my son. He is your greatest enemy."

Thowra could not really remember the man who had tried to catch him as he slept on the slopes of the Ramshead Range, but that day had planted the fear of Man deeply in him. All he said now was:

"Let's go!"

They moved away quietly, and that evening, as they grazed with the herd by a wide creek bed, where good grass grew, Bel Bel and Mirri told Yarraman and the gathered mares and yearlings what they had seen.

"I don't like it," said Bel Bel. "He was a mountain man and he will have come here for some purpose, not just curiosity."

"They are sure to know that many of us always spend the summer here," Mirri said. "It wouldn't be good if they came back to hunt us."

"We know this country too well," boasted Yarraman, but he did not look overpleased.

The two mares kept an even more careful watch on their foals, and would never let them go down to the river except very early and very late when men who live in huts or tents are always busy with their queer cans of water that bubble by their smoking fires.

Once again, the man was seen, this time by Yarraman himself as he and the herd were in their customary grazing ground. The man was standing right above them as though he were cut out of rock.

The news of this was very disquieting to Bel Bel and Mirri, and they kept an even stricter watch.

There were many hot, sleepy days that summer, but though the foals lay in the grass, flat out, their switching tails their only sign of life, the two mothers kept watch in turns, never, during the day, sleeping at the same time. Even so, they were both sleepy enough, standing in the shade of a low snowgum, to get badly frightened when they heard an unusual noise far below them.

What was it? Something was moving through dead timber the way no wild animal would move! Perhaps a tame horse with a man on its back?

They could not smell anything. Nostrils to the wind, they listened. There was the sound again, something unusual going through the bush, they were sure. They roused the sleeping foals and began to move quietly upwards.

When Thowra made to jump up on a large rocky outcrop, Bel Bel nipped him and pushed him back.

"Don't be so silly," she said, "making yourself a clear mark for anyone to see! Keep in the trees and keep quiet."

Sometimes they stopped to listen, but for a while there was no sound except that of a kurrawong and the chatter of gang gangs in the trees. Then, during one such stop, they heard a faint sound of movement, so faint that no one except those who lived in the bush would have heard it, and they knew it was something wild like themselves. Presently three silver-grey kangaroos went hopping by.

Thowra and Storm were delighted to see them, but both Bel Bel and Mirri looked worried. Not long afterwards, they saw four young colts making up the hill too.

They came to a small clear stream where the foals wanted to play.

"Have a drink, but not too much, and come on," said Bel Bel. Three black cockatoos flew out of the trees by the water, with their weird, wild crying, and the foals jumped back, startled.

Mirri looked back fearfully.

"Something's happening, I'm sure," she muttered.

Even a gust of wind rustling the shiny leaves made the mares start nervously, then they saw some of their own herd heading towards their main camping ground which was in an unexpected hanging valley not far from the top of the range. They caught up to these mares and foals, and Bel Bel said:

"Have you seen anything strange as you travelled homewards at midday?"

One was Star's dam, and she answered fearfully:

"No, but we heard the sound of horsemen and a faint whip crack. What business have men here?"

Then through the bush, some distance off, they saw several more kangaroos flitting between the trees, upwards, upwards.

Bel Bel turned to Mirri.

"We're being driven uphill," she said. "There must be a great many men."

"Well, we're going," said Star's mother. "We'll be safer with Yarraman and the others."

Bel Bel looked at Mirri.

"It must be us wild horses they're after, not kangaroos," she said.

"Good luck!" said Mirri to the others, as they jogged away, then to Bel Bel, "Shall we try to go across the hill and escape the men?"

"That's the best thing I can think of. We might make the ravine and hide there, but the men will probably have dogs and though *we* might race them, it's not going to be so easy with the foals – but we must go." And, as usual, the creamy mare led off, the two foals following her, and Mirri close behind them.

All of a sudden, the bush seemed dreadfully still and hot, so hot, and the scent of the turpentine bush was all around. Bel Bel leapt to one side sharply as a big copperhead snake slid across some warm, bare earth almost under her feet, and she felt the sweat break out behind her ears.

Coming up the hill towards her she saw a pair of brown wallabies.

"Yes, we're being driven," she whispered to herself.

Further on they met more brumbies, panting and sweating. The leader only stopped for a second to say to them:

"You'll meet stockmen if you keep going that way. They're not far behind. Better follow us."

"There are men everywhere," said Bel Bel. "The only thing to do is to try and get back between them."

But the other horses just went on upwards, their flanks heaving and the smell of their sweat heavy on the air.

Bel Bel led off again, faster, threading through thick snowgums, even breaking into a fast canter when they reached a grass glade. As much as possible she avoided rocks on which their hooves would make a noise. If only they could reach the ravine...

Then she saw the first of the men, sitting easily on a neat grey horse, a Queensland blue cattle dog padding along beside him.

She doubled back quickly, driving Thowra and Storm in front of her. Perhaps he had not seen her. Perhaps he would not hear them. If they went back a few hundred yards, and then turned downwards, they might just get through the cordon of men and dogs... but when she turned down, there, galloping across in front of her, was the same man and his dog.

The dog saw the wild horses and rushed to head them, snapping not at her or Mirri, who might have kicked, but at Thowra.

Thowra, who had never seen a dog in his life, turned in a frenzy of fear. Bel Bel galloped after him, trying to swing him back to make another effort to beat the man and the dog downhill, but the dog knew his game too well and kept heeling Thowra. Thowra was soon beyond being able to hear anything his mother neighed to him, and all that Bel Bel could do was to go with him in his mad gallop up the hill, trying to strike or kick at the dog. At last she quietened the blue heeler by galloping at him when he snapped at Thowra's heel and giving him a nasty bite on the back.

Bel Bel then galloped shoulder to shoulder with Thowra, speaking to him, trying to steady him, and all the time wondering what they should do next. In a few quick, backward glances she could see no sign of Mirri and Storm. The man was a good way behind and had called off his dog. Anyway, the dog had done his job of heading them uphill only too well.

She gave Thowra a gentle nip on the shoulder.

"Slow down!" she said. "They are not following."

Thowra, who was blowing frightfully, slackened his pace and at last dropped to a walk.

"We will have a little rest in that thick belt of snowgums," Bel Bel said, "and, from there, try and cut across to the ravine again." But the time had gone for escape. The men and their dogs were closing in.

Bel Bel found herself and her foal driven relentlessly uphill. Each time she hoped to cut across she saw a man. Presently they came up with several trembling mares and foals, and they could hear others moving on ahead. Bel Bel made one more bid to break away south to the ravine, but just then she heard a whip crack, and another, from the direction of the ravine, and some more brumbies came galloping towards her.

"Don't try to go that way," they said. "Lots of men and dogs there. Quick, quick!" and they galloped on in terror.

Bel Bel realized that they were all being swung round in the direction of their main camping ground.

"The men will have made a yard somewhere," she

thought, because this was not the first time she had been caught up in a big hunt when the stockmen came after the brumbies. She wished Mirri was still with her. Mirri was a good friend, and she understood more about the habits of men. Mirri would know where they would build a yard in which to catch wild horses. As for Bel Bel she could think of no place more likely than in the narrow mouth of the valley at its farthest end.

She tried to talk to Thowra before he got completely infected with the panic that was gripping all the other horses.

"Son," she said, "you must stay absolutely beside me. Somewhere these men will have put up fences with which to stop us escaping. If you stay right with me, I may be able just to miss going into their yard and we might escape."

Thowra thought he would never forget all that happened after that. First he heard sticks and branches breaking as though hundreds of men and horses were chasing them, then he heard the unknown ring of a shod horse's hoof on stone, and *then* whips cracking, many whips, cracking and cracking, right behind them.

The brumbies really started to gallop, and he and his mother with them.

The little foal stretched his legs out beside his mother, stretched his neck too. He could feel his heart thundering unevenly in his chest. They were right in the centre of the mob. It was Brownie's shoulder that touched him on his near side, and he felt her hot breath. Everything was bound up with the tremendous pounding, thundering of hooves on hard ground, the pounding and thundering of his own heart, the blowing of breath, the gasping of all the horses.

A snowgum branch whipped him across the eyes, and brought stinging tears. He could hear his own breath sob and felt as though his pounding heart would burst. His legs and hooves seemed no longer to belong to him.

Then they were out of the trees and they spread apart a little in the open valley of the camping ground. The men forced them together again into a mob that moved almost as one horse, but, while they were spread out, Thowra had felt Bel Bel pushing him over to the left wing, not quite on the outside of the mob, because their colour would be too noticeable there, but just near the edge. He heard his mother give a gasping sort of whinny, and, through the tired haze that was over his eyes, recognized Mirri and Storm on the wing.

The noise of whips never ceased now, as the men drove them faster and faster. The horses were in a frenzy of fear. Thowra wanted to cry out with the terror that seemed to run like a flame through the mob, but he had no breath for anything except to keep going. Bel Bel spoke to him several times and he hardly heard. Then he knew she was saying something that mattered.

"In a second we will swing to the left," she said, "through the gap in the trees."

With a tremendous effort he focused his eyes on something other than the outstretched noses and heaving flanks beside him, and saw that they were nearly at the end of the valley.

"Now!" said Bel Bel, and edged him out of the mob, neighing to Mirri as they went.

Only a few strides and they would be in the trees. Thowra realized it was Storm beside him and that the two mares were driving them. He felt a searing cut across the face from a whip. A dog fastened on his heel and he heard Bel Bel's scream of rage, but his mother and Mirri forced him on.

There was a jumble of men's voices, one calling:

"Hold the ones we've got!" Another singing out: "No! I swear I'll have the creamies."

Then they were in the trees and pounding over rocks, one man and his dog still with them. Bel Bel raced into the lead and Thowra suddenly knew why. There was quite a drop ahead of them, over some rocks. He and Storm had played there often and knew just where to jump. All at once he felt strong enough to go at the faster pace that his mother was setting.

Bel Bel leapt over the edge, jumping on to a little rocky shelf, sliding down from it on her haunches, jumping again, and he was following, legs trembling so much that he could barely stand up when he landed.

Standing at the foot of the little cliff, legs apart, shaking, shaking, he looked up. Mirri and Storm were nearly safely down, but the man had reined in on the top and was left behind.

"Come on," said Bel Bel, and the four brumbies vanished into the trees.

Cassowary

Chapter Five

MAN, THE INVADER

THAT NIGHT THE weather changed suddenly. Stars faded under cloud, a whining wind crept around the rock tors and down the grassy lanes between the snowgums. Far up on the range, the dingoes howled.

Where Mirri and Bel Bel and their two foals lay, there was no other sound except the whining wind and the dingoes, but nearer the top of the range there were rustlings and stealthy movements. Kangaroos that had been driven from their usual haunts were carefully looking around and starting home again. Birds were disturbed and anxious, unable to settle for the night. Brumbies who had escaped the hunt or broken out of the yard, footsore and exhausted, moved fearfully into the back country.

A large camp fire blazed in the grassy valley and nearly a dozen men slept around it. In the rough yard they had built, there were about fifteen brumbies. There would have been more, but a great heavy colt, in trying to jump out, had smashed one corner of the yard, and quite a few, including Brownie and Arrow, had escaped. Yarraman and others of the herd had never been in the original round-up.

All night long the brumbies trapped in the yard neighed and called, walked and walked, and neighed. Rain came in fitful showers, hissing in the fire, steaming on the brumbies' sweating coats. Raindrops woke Bel Bel and Mirri, who were barely sleeping anyway, but no raindrop could have disturbed the two exhausted foals. They slept deeply, occasionally half-neighing at the ugliness of a dream.

During the next day they lay quietly hidden in thick snowgums and hop scrub by a water soak where the wombats and shy brown wallabies came to drink. They could hear the noise of whips and voices, but knew that it was only the sound of the preparations the men were now making to take the brumbies away with them. It was very unlikely that there would be any more hunting unless the creamies were seen, so it was better to lie low till the men had gone.

Before midday, the sounds of whip cracks had become far distant and by afternoon the bush had returned to its usual silence – silence that is not silence but the blend of water music, the sound of wind, of moving branches and moving soft-footed animals, and the song of birds. All that was different was the hanging smell of smoke; and there, in the camping valley was the trampled, spoiled grass, the dead fire, and the hidden remains of the trap-yard.

Bel Bel and Mirri did not go to see what was left; they took their foals and skirted round the valley to the north and east, searching till they found brumby tracks, and the tracks of Yarraman himself.

Yarraman's tracks were over a day old, but there were fresher ones – Thowra gave a squeal as he found Brownie's and Arrow's – and they followed along the tracks for some miles till Yarraman had apparently deliberately gone over a great rough cliff of rock and stone, where no track would remain.

"I know where he's gone," said Bel Bel. "He will have headed for the Hidden Flat," and she struck off across the cliff.

It was evening when they reached a narrow, grassy flat deep down in a gorge. Since the walls of the gorge were so steep, and the trees on its side so tall, no one approaching could see down into the Hidden Flat, and they did not know if the others were still there till they reached the grass. Then they heard a welcoming neigh from Yarraman as he came trotting to meet them.

The herd stayed around the Hidden Flat till the days grew shorter, the nights frosty and bright; till the rivers were stilled with the cold, and shining so that one could see each stone clearly in the bottom, and every reflection infinitely clear and yet deep, so deep. Then the wild things in the mountains knew that the snow must be coming soon and the stockmen would be too busy mustering their cattle to have any more brumby hunts. It was safe to go back to Paddy Rush's Bogong and listen and watch over the other side of the Crackenback for the going of the herds, when they could return to the Cascades for the winter and spring.

Thowra and Storm had both grown a lot, but Arrow was still the biggest of all the foals. He was arrogant and mean-minded, but, since Thowra and Storm had so easily lost him in the clouds and brought him ignominiously home again, he had left them in peace from petty bites and kicks.

The other foals had learnt to hate him and yet rather to admire him, but, while Thowra and Storm knew the country better than he, and knew all the signs and sounds of the bush, Arrow, even though he was bigger, stronger, and faster, could never be acknowledged leader of the foals. Also it was well known among the mares that Yarraman admired Bel Bel and Mirri and never bossed them around like he did the others: after all, mares that could fend for themselves and who knew the mountains better than he did could hardly be bossed by a stallion.

Autumn was a happy time for Thowra and Storm and their mothers.

The brumbies listened to the sounds of herds of cattle being mustered above the Crackenback, and finally saw that the last bullock and the last man had left the mountains, and there was no more smoke coming from the chimneys of the huts. Thowra and Storm were as eager as any of them to cross the shining Crackenback and climb back upwards to return to their barely remembered old home at the Cascades — to find again the great wide valley of springy snowgrass where one could gallop and gallop.

Wombat

Chapter Six

INVISIBLE IN SNOW

THOWRA AND STORM were naturally very frightened of men and dogs since they had been hunted, but they were also very curious.

After they had been some weeks in the Cascades, they gathered up their courage and climbed on to the little knoll where the slab and shingle stockman's hut stood above the creek. Though it had been empty for a long time now, there were still strange smells lurking round it, and some salt spilt on the ground, which they licked up. Salt was good. There were natural salt-licks in the bush, but not many of them, and sometimes one could find a little left round the places where the men salted their cattle.

Thowra sniffed all round the hut looking – looking for something, he didn't know what. The cold wind blew a tin billy that had been left hanging under the eaves of the hut.

He jumped backwards and Storm snorted with amusement.

"Come away," he said. "There is nothing here. The sky looks very queer, and the others are a long way off."

The wind rustled the golden everlastings that grew in the grass about their feet, and in the trees close by its low moaning sounded.

"The clouds seem heavy," said Storm, "as though they are pressing down. I never remember a day like this before."

"O stupid one," said Thowra with a toss of his head. "You've never lived through a winter before. Mother said we must not go too far today because of the weather, but let us just go and listen to the sound the wind is making in the big trees."

There were some tall trees, candlebarks and the first of the great mountain ash, near the Cascades hut, and the two foals had already discovered the fun of playing "Tug-you-last" around the great tree-trunks and up and down the clear glades. Now, as soon as they were in the timber, they could hear the wail of the wind in the tree-tops, far above, and the soughing and sighing of streamers of bark that hung down the trunks.

They felt very small and alone – and very excited.

"What was that?" asked Thowra nervously, as something white and feathery floated down from the dark sky and landed, freezing cold, on his nose.

Storm jumped to one side and shook his head as another cold white feather fell on his ear. They cantered away under a big tree, but, even there, floating so slowly and lightly on the air, the white feathers came, in ones and twos at first but thicker and thicker till the air was filled with floating whiteness.

It was a long time before they thought of looking at the ground.

"Look!" cried Storm. "It is even making the ground white. We should go home. Perhaps it will be difficult to find our way."

It was all right while they were in among the tall trees and had the trunks to guide them, but out in the open valley all was a blinding whirl of blown whiteness. The shape of tracks could still be seen, and Thowra jogged along one, his nose to the ground. Storm ran right beside him, almost bumping into him.

"You will tread on me," Thowra complained. "What is the matter?"

"I can hardly see you in this queer white stuff," said Storm, and he sounded afraid. His own dark coat showed up clearly, but Thowra was almost invisible.

Thowra looked around him then and felt half-afraid too. Nothing could be seen except the swirling, whirling flakes; no contours of hill or ridge, not even the loops of the streams, but the hollow of track still showed just at his feet.

"Quick, we must follow it before it gets buried," he said. "By then we should be at the creek."

When they reached the stream they stopped to watch the strange white flakes which almost hissed as they touched the water – and then vanished.

They waded through the ice-cold water and followed the stream on the other bank, knowing they should soon come to the little creek that flowed down from the herd's camping valley.

They kept shaking their heads to try and free their eyelashes and nostrils of the queer white stuff. Their forelocks, solid and wet, hit their eyes with each shake.

When they had gone a little way Thowra suddenly stopped, raised his head and neighed loudly. He could see nothing at all but the white storm, but ahead came answering neighs and he broke into a canter. Bel Bel and Mirri had come down to the junction of the valley to wait for them.

They could see Mirri from several yards off, but were almost on top of Bel Bel before they saw her.

"What's happening to the world, Mother?" asked Thowra, feeling very glad to be safely with her.

"Why, this is a snowstorm, Son. It's heavy for early in the winter," she said, her voice worried, "and it's heavy for down here. We may go hungry before the spring."

The two mares led their foals back to the herd who were huddled together in the shelter of some trees. There they spent the cold, stormy night, with the wind howling and the snow lying thick on their warm coats.

By morning the snow had stopped falling but it lay nearly a foot deep on the ground. Trees were bowed down with it, each leaf coated in white crystals. There was no grass to eat unless one scratched away the snow with a hoof.

Disconsolately, the herd wandered down into the main valley.

"The sun will come out soon," said Bel Bel, "and then the snow will thaw and we will have grass to eat again."

When the sun did come out and warm them, all the foals soon found that they could have great fun chasing each other up and down the glittering white hills.

Thowra was no longer invisible, now that the air was clear of the wind-swivelled flakes, but somehow the snow seemed to be his kingdom, and the other foals soon saw that he was swifter and more sure-footed in it than Arrow. Of course if one knew where every hole or little watercourse was, one did not make any stupid mistakes. Arrow forgot that there was a little tiny stream at the foot of one ridge. He went galloping down, chasing Thowra and never noticed Thowra's flying leap at the bottom. His forefeet broke through the snow into the creek and, in a wild flurry of snow, he turned a complete somersault, finishing up almost buried.

Thowra saw exactly what happened, and by the time Arrow had got to his feet, shaken all the snow out of his eyes and ears, and gingerly tested his legs, Thowra was rearing and neighing on top of a high rock on the next ridge.

If Arrow had had any sense, he would have taken no notice, but he got in a fury of anger at the sight of the beautiful creamy, who was almost white now, in his thick winter coat, his silver mane and tail gleaming and glittering in the sun, as he pranced and reared.

Arrow made after him, with all the watching foals, neighing and snorting, kicking and pawing up the snow.

Thowra waited until the chestnut was three strides away from the back of the rock, then he reared up and pirouetted on his hind legs, gave a squeal of joy, and leapt off the steep side of the rocks on to the soft snow, then away down the ridge, bucking and snorting.

Bel Bel and Mirri were at the bottom.

"That's enough, my son. You are making a bad enemy for yourself," said Bel Bel, but she had enjoyed Thowra's pranks, and there was a gleam of pleasure in her eyes. Her cream colt had looked so joyously beautiful rearing up on the snow-covered rock. "Come now," she went on, "we will go down the mountainside a little way and see if we can find some food."

Mirri called Storm and off the four of them went, down the valley and into the tall timber where Storm and Thowra had watched the start of the snowfall the day before. Here Thowra suddenly stopped dead, snorting at the ground. Right at his nose was a set of fresh tracks in the snow, little tracks just like a child's bare feet, but the foals did not know that. Where the snow was very soft and deep, there was a gutter in between the feetmarks.

Bel Bel and Mirri said nothing when the foals began following the trail, noses down. Suddenly Thowra, who was leading, stopped and nearly sat back on his haunches with fright. Only a yard or two ahead of him was the round, furry back of a wombat who was grubbing for food. The wombat took no notice whatever but just went on grubbing through snow and mud with his sharp little nose. Bel Bel and Mirri watched, their muzzles twitching a little.

Thowra stood up and stretched out his neck to sniff the thick fur. The wombat turned round surprisingly fast, his beady eyes angry. Thowra nearly sat down again, as the wombat waddled on, his round, fat middle making the gutter in the snow.

The horses kept jogging on downwards, nibbling at wattles and odd shrubs. At last, when the snow got thinner, they turned off the spur on to the northern slope where, as the mare well knew they would, they found tussocks of snowgrass.

That night as they camped by a clear singing stream, Bel Bel sniffed the air and looked at the sky.

"There'll be a frost tonight," she said, "and another fine day, but I can't help feeling there's going to be a lot of snow, and we'll have to find somewhere else to winter, lower than the Cascades."

"Well, the nearest lower country with good grass belongs to The Brolga," said Mirri.

Storm and Thowra both pricked up their ears.

The Native Cat

Chapter Seven

SEEKING GRASS

HEAVY FROSTS MADE ice on the creeks and froze small, still pools quite solid. In the wonderful bright days that came after each frost, though some of the more weather-wise mares might be worrying about the hard winter that was coming, the foals played and had mock fights with wild exuberance. The biting cold and the bright sun, as Mirri said, had put the devil into them.

Then one day, after an iron-hard frost, clouds came up before the dawn and a moaning, icy wind came from the north. Just as the grey light crept over the valley a flock of black cockatoos flew screaming, crying, to the south, borne on the wind.

"Hmph," said Bel Bel to Yarraman. "I don't like it."

Yarraman looked as if he had not heard her, but as the light grew stronger he started grazing his way into the main valley and then south-east – just steadily south-east all day, without haste, but never turning back.

The clouds grew heavier and darker, the wind colder. No ice melted that day.

"We haven't seen any other horses," Thowra heard his mother whisper to Mirri. "The Brolga must have already decided to go to his lower pastures."

That night they sheltered in an unaccustomed valley and just at nightfall the snow started to beat down in the wind.

The herd moved around under the trees all night, stamping and whinnying softly. Sometimes a foal dropped down on the hard, cold ground and slept; mostly the sense of disquiet throughout the whole herd kept even the young ones from sleeping soundly.

Thowra did not know what made him feel excited and yet afraid. He did not realize that his mother's anxiety since the first heavy snowfall had been communicating itself to him, or that the strange feeling which all the grown horses had slowly begun to get – that a hard winter was coming – had somehow made everyone touchy, apt to gallop, kick, or bite. He only knew that the howl of the wind and the cold lash of the snow made him want to gallop now, even in the pitch darkness, and leap on to a high rock, rear and neigh loudly to the sky. He could imagine the wild neigh ringing out and the thought of it sent cold shivers down his backbone.

Suddenly he realized that Arrow was passing him and he lashed out with his heels. Arrow gave a squeal of rage and pain but Thowra had cantered off into the storm and the night. Unable to bear his own feelings any longer, he lifted his head to the falling snow and neighed with all his strength. There was a sudden hushed silence in the herd, and then from far to the south-east came an answering, distant neigh.

Thowra stiffened, tingling with a mad excitement, but Bel Bel came up at his side then, and she nipped him on the wither.

"Be quiet, silly one," she said, not unkindly. "Yarraman will punish you if you make too much noise. Don't you realize we are no longer in our own country, and that he may have to fight for our food?"

"Are we in The Brolga's country?" Thowra was quivering with nervousness.

"Yes, we are, and we will have to go further into it yet, to get out of the heavy snow."

"I wish daylight would come."

"The winter nights are long," said Bel Bel. "Sleep while I stand beside you. Tomorrow you may have to fight Arrow for that kick you gave him. We may travel a long way too. You will need your strength."

When the dawn came, grey and beating with hard, wind-driven snow, Yarraman led off immediately, still south-east, but upwards, over a gap in the hills.

There were strange horse tracks at the mouth of a small valley. Yarraman sniffed them curiously but went on his own way. Bel Bel and Mirri both branched off up the little valley for a few yards, looking carefully at the tracks.

"No more than four young horses, I should think," Bel Bel said. "Certainly The Brolga is not with them."

Just in the few minutes while they looked at the tracks,

the herd had vanished into the storm and their tracks were fast getting covered. Thowra and Storm were both quite bothered, but Bel Bel and Mirri trotted upwards, and kept trotting till the herd came into sight, shadow horses behind a dense curtain of flying snow.

All day long the wind howled and drove the snow in this impenetrable curtain. Often the horses were almost carried along by the wind.

They were getting hungry now, and the only water they had was when they broke the ice on a pool. The foals demanded, and got, milk from their mothers, but there would not be much milk if they had to keep going like this, driven on the storm, and never finding grass. Even the mares were tiring, perhaps because the cold was so intense, and if they stopped they got colder still.

At last, when they had gone a long way down the other side of the gap, Yarraman turned into a side valley that ran across the wind and had plenty of trees for shelter, and there they spent another restless, anxious night.

At dawn the storm still swirled and beat around them. They set off again, cold, tired, and hungry, and filled with a dread of staying still in one place. They were still steadily losing height and both the ground and the air must have been warmer than it was in the Cascades because the snow was wetter and not as thick on the ground.

They came, at last, to flatter ground in what seemed to be a basin into which flowed quite a number of streams. Yarraman went several miles downstream and then he started fossicking around for shrubs to eat and the odd patch of grass that might be sticking out of the snow underneath a tree.

"It looks as if this is where we're going to stop," Mirri said to Bel Bel. Bel Bel was staring at the bank of the stream: snow lay right to the water's edge, but just where there was a crossing there were still the shapes of hoof-marks half-filled with snow.

"Hmn!" she said, peering more closely and then crossing over and looking at the other side. "Hmn! Quite a few horses have crossed fairly recently I think." She scratched away some snow from the bank and found muddied, tracked snow underneath.

"Well, what of it?" asked Mirri. "We've got to eat, and we may eat better here than higher up."

"Looks as if it will be a quarrelsome winter," Bel Bel said, and she turned her head towards Yarraman. A hard winter would not worry a horse approaching his prime, like The Brolga, but Yarraman would feel it. The Brolga would not have attained full strength yet, but he must be getting very near it. "Anyway," she went on, "nothing is likely to happen during such a blizzard. Everyone will be too taken up with finding food."

The blizzard continued for days. Sometimes, down in the low valley, the snow turned to rain, then it would snow again. The horses managed to find bushes which they could eat, and, though they were hungry, they were not desperate.

Now that they were no longer travelling, but wandering around trying to find food, Thowra thought he would be able to have some fun, particularly annoying Arrow, since he himself would be almost invisible in the flying snow, but he found it so difficult to see his own mother that he never liked to get far away from her in case he lost her in the blizzard and in the unknown country.

Once, Bel Bel left him with Mirri while she went off scouting further down the stream, and, by the importance of her behaviour, Thowra felt sure Yarraman had asked her to go and see what she could see. In that time, he sneaked away from Mirri, crept up on Arrow and gave him a playful nip, but he could not help feeling afraid of the rough weather and the constantly falling snow, and he was glad when his mother came home, even though she had absolutely nothing interesting to tell them.

At last there came a day when the snow stopped falling, and the following night, close on midnight, the wind dropped. Thowra woke because of the sudden silence when there was no longer the howl of the wind, and in that silence he heard, far away but echoing, the shrill trumpeting neigh of a stallion.

He scrambled to his feet and was just going to neigh in tremulous answer when Bel Bel gave him a swift nip.

"Why, oh why, have I got such an excitable son?" she said, half in anger, half in pride. "It is not your place to answer that call," and just then Yarraman's wild cry rang out.

There was an instant's electric silence; not one of the herd moved or let go a breath. Then, faraway again, but shrill with anger, came the stallion cry.

"Tomorrow will start the fights for the grass that we haven't found yet," said Mirri acidly.

"And the youngest, lightest horse will have an advantage in this snow," Bel Bel added.

The foals dropped off to sleep again, but there was a restless lack of ease among the mares and young colts and fillies.

Not long after the grey dawn, The Brolga and some of his mares appeared out of the mist and clouds.

Yarraman pranced forward out from his herd, stepping high, head up imperiously, tail held high and free.

Along came The Brolga, rearing and screaming.

A shock of excitement ran through the herd. The Brolga was growing into a noble horse; yet their own Yarraman was superb – like a sun god against the grey clouds and white snow.

Thowra shivered. The Brolga, like his mother and himself, had that queer quality of merging with snow and cloud. In a real fight that might prove an advantage over the bright chestnut.

He could smell the two stallions' anger and excitement as they went to meet each other; there was a roar from both horses as they reached within striking distance. Then the snow was flying from their hooves as they circled each other, striking, biting, screaming. Thowra saw blood staining the snow, and the mud and the snow and the blood churned underfoot.

Yarraman had The Brolga in a terrific grip with his teeth, but suddenly the older horse's hooves slipped in the snow and he was forced to let go. Round and round they circled again. The nimbler, lighter Brolga could certainly keep his feet better and when Yarraman slipped again, he managed to get a cruel hold just above the chestnut's wither. Screaming with rage and pain, Yarraman lashed out and missed him, and then with a tremendous effort shook himself free and planted both heels in The Brolga's chest, almost winding him.

The Brolga had a gash above one eye, too, where Yarraman had struck. It half-blinded him, but he could still move more lightly and surely than the heavier horse. Now, each was trying for the deadly grip on the wither. Yarraman succeeded, but now he was so breathless that the watching herd could see that, even if he defeated the younger horse *this* time, he would not have the wind to give him a real beating.

Thowra looked with horror at all the blood on the snow, and at the two exhausted horses, and when Yarraman let go, for want of strength to hold on any longer, he found himself hoping and hoping that The Brolga would have no fighting strength left either.

With relief he saw the great grey horse backing off, every muscle trembling with exhaustion, backing, backing, his one good eye never leaving Yarraman who stood, a huge, bleeding statue, in front of his mares.

Dingo Dog

Chapter Eight

NEW WISDOM

YARRAMAN HAD WON the right for himself and his herd to eat what food they could find when the snow melted, but each mare knew that they could peacefully graze only just as long as they did not trespass on any territory on which The Brolga and his herd were grazing.

Throughout the winter there were several fights between the young colts that ran with each herd, but the two stallions kept away from each other, and let their wounds heal.

Yarraman's took a long time to heal up. Perhaps the food was not good enough to keep his blood strong; perhaps it was just that the snow had got into the wounds. No one knew how soon The Brolga had recovered, only Thowra saw him once, standing high upon a rock, looking out over a snowy landscape – and, to Thowra, he looked vital, and strong, and terrifying.

It *was* a hard winter, snow fell often and the great winds roared down from the higher mountains. There was very little food.

Sometimes Thowra and Storm found a stream that danced and bubbled under its shimmering cover of ice; sometimes hoar frost fringed grass and leaves and made the lovely ice flowers on the frozen pools. Sometimes they heard the song the wind played on the ice-encased snowgum leaves.

Bel Bel and Mirri would not let them wander far away for fear of meeting the other herd, even they themselves wandered less than usual, afraid of bringing trouble on themselves and Yarraman. But when some instinct told Bel Bel that a great deal of the snow must have gone from the Cascades, she and Mirri and their foals set off for home without waiting for the others.

It was far from being springtime and the grass was flattened and lifeless, but the two mares and Thowra and Storm felt very happy to be home again. There was still a lot of snow in the Cascades, but it was patchy and plum-duffed with earth and grass. Their usual end of the valley was more heavily snowed than the southern end in which the foals had first seen The Brolga, so they mostly grazed there in The Brolga's country.

Plenty of sunny days came and nights of heavy frost. Once, in a deep cleft in the hills, they found the rustling leaf snow, like Lux flakes, and Thowra and Storm descended the cleft magnificently, rolling and wriggling on their backs, the separate, shining icy leaves tossing over them, rising in spume.

"You, who are nearly yearlings, play like babies," snorted Bel Bel, and lay down and rolled herself.

Sometimes the mares' wanderlust would take them far up into the snow on Bob's Ridge and they would all four chase each other downwards, ploughing through the snow, galloping and falling. Then one day they arrived back in the Cascades to find that the herd had returned. Thowra and Storm were not even sure they were pleased to see them — it had been such fun on their own.

Brownie gave Bel Bel a spiteful look when she saw them.

"You two'll turn your foals into lone wolves like yourselves," she said. "And you'll each one of you probably meet a bad end."

"We'll have had a good life, though." Bel Bel bared her teeth at Brownie.

It was only a few days after that that Thowra and Arrow had their first real fight and finished bruised and cut, with neither victorious. Thowra came away a little wiser; he knew his mother had been right, that he had made a vindictive enemy in Arrow and that maybe there would be many fights.

"Spring will be late this year," Bel Bel said, on one of the many days when cold winds swept the valley. "I am glad I am not having a foal this time."

As it was, only one foal had been born. Then on a day when the breeze was soft and warm, and the sun shone brightly, then did the mares realize that Yarraman's coat, and their own, were beginning to get a gloss on them again — that spring had come.

★ ★ ★

Spring had come and the robin redbreasts were up in the snow, hunting the black insects; the dingoes howled to their mates in the full moon at nights. Then one day there was the sound of a wild stallion screaming, farther to the south.

Yarraman pricked up his ears and listened and when the scream came again, unmistakably, he threw up his head with the lovely cream and gold mane and roared his wild answer. As the sun got higher, he trotted a little way up on to a ridge to watch The Brolga, standing with his head well in the air, and the sunlight glinting on his coat. Sometimes he would call out a challenge, but The Brolga did not come. Yarraman would reign, that spring, undisputed king of the Cascade brumbies.

So the foals became yearlings and, in the good spring and summer that followed the snowy winter, they grew large and strong, and learnt to gallop much faster. It took Arrow a long time to realize that though he was the biggest of them all, and the strongest, Thowra was living up to his name and could travel like the wind, faster than himself or any of the others.

There were no organized brumby hunts that summer, but Thowra learnt to recognize – and dread – the whistling sound of a rope flying through the air, and once felt the rough blow of it as it glanced off his shoulder. As Bel Bel had known he would, the beautiful cream colt attracted any man that saw him, and, in his strength and brave courage, he did not seek to hide himself in the same way as she did.

She tried to teach him all her cunning, but realized she could not expect him to learn everything in one short year.

Storm became a faster mover, too, and the mares were proud of them both – watched them grow more and more independent throughout the summer and autumn; watched with pleasure how the friendship between the two remained as staunch as ever. They saw, too, the enmity increase between Arrow and Thowra, and wondered what the outcome would be.

In the two colts' second winter the snow did not fall heavily or continuously in the Cascades, and the herd were able to stay there.

Both Thowra and Storm saw The Brolga several times and knew that he was now a superb horse. Thowra told Bel Bel, once, that he had seen him and she said:

"With the spring grass and sunshine, and the mating season, he will reach the height of his strength and agility," but she said no more, and left the young horse wondering.

Towards the end of the winter, Thowra saw less and less of his mother, and he and Storm ran more with the other young colts, biting and fighting, galloping, feeling a sudden restlessness. Spring was coming once again and they were almost two-year-olds. Now, Bel Bel and Mirri were both in foal, and they went off to higher slopes where they could have their foals undisturbed. The young colts went wandering farther and farther afield, sometimes returning to the herd, sometimes spending a night in other country.

There were about six or eight two-year-olds rapidly becoming independent of the herd. Sometimes Thowra and Storm ran with them. Sometimes they, the lone wolves, went off on their own, but they were all together and grazing not far from the main herd up a narrow valley the evening Bel Bel came back with her chestnut foal.

Thowra was beginning to move inquisitively nearer when he heard a clamour that made the sweat break out on his gleaming coat, and he knew that it was the challenge to the leader of the brumbies which, in a way, he had expected.

The Brolga came high-stepping up the valley.

Mopoke

Chapter Nine

FIGHT TO THE DEATH

YARRAMAN SCREAMED HIS wild answer to The Brolga's challenge, the rock and hillside echoing it until it rolled in the gullies. Again, in a spring evening, he went galloping, with streaming golden mane and tail, to meet the grey Brolga, but this time The Brolga was no immature young horse, but a magnificent stallion, just at his prime.

For the third time − and perhaps the last − Thowra watched the grey and the chestnut advancing to within striking distance, watched their swirling, whirling, purposeful dance, saw the bared teeth, heard the screams of rage. In each fight The Brolga had had the advantage of seeming to melt into the oncoming night or the snowstorm.

The noise of the fight echoed in a terrible way so that the screams of the two horses were doubled or trebled, and only the closest of the watchers could hear the tremendous pounding of their hooves on the ground.

Thowra and Storm had drawn apart from the other young colts, watching fearfully while the two stallions struggled for mastery. There would be no mercy given by either, and, as night drew on, they knew darkness would not part them.

Yarraman was the first to get a deadly grip above The Brolga's withers but the younger horse managed at last to free himself and at the same time strike Yarraman in the eyes. They fought on and on, not screaming so often now, but their breath snorting through red, dilated nostrils. And all the time the darkness was coming up the valley.

Then suddenly the watchers saw The Brolga, in turn, get his grip on Yarraman; they saw Yarraman's valiant struggles repeated and repeated; they saw that he could not free himself, and, as night fell, they could just see him beaten to his knees.

Suddenly there was a scream of triumph from The Brolga as he struck blow after blow with his forefeet at the stallion on the ground. Then, in the darkness, they could see the pale shadow of The Brolga and the dark shadow on the ground, hear the pounding of hooves on flesh.

Shuddering, the young horses drew back; the mares, snorting their terror, took their foals away. Down in the broader valley, by the first faint light of a rising moon, Thowra could see the pale form of Bel Bel. Then there was a thunder of galloping hooves and The Brolga was among them. They could smell his sweat, see his pale outline, all stained with dark. Thowra watched him go straight up to Bel Bel, nickering out the greeting of a victorious stallion. To every man and beast her colour – and his – must be attractive. He felt himself sweating with fear again.

Thowra, and the other colts, turned away and left the herd, heading towards the edge of the tall timber, with no idea where to go, but urgently wanting to escape. They stopped in a little field of snowgrass, just inside the first fringe of trees, and there they spent the night, no longer playing at being independent, but young colts without a herd.

When the moon was high, without even disturbing Storm, Thowra slid away through the trees. The moonlight was very bright in the main valley; he looked carefully around before he moved out of the sheltering trees, then he walked into the bright, cold light that made his coat as silver as his mane and tail. A mopoke called mournfully; he jumped, but did not draw back. On he went till he was going up the narrow valley in which they had all been that evening. Presently he climbed on to a high rock and looked round the bend of the valley below him. There lay the great bulk of Yarraman, dark on the ground.

Suddenly there was a noise beside him and another horse came out of the shadows and joined him on his rock.

"Thowra, my son," said Bel Bel's voice softly, as she climbed up alongside, herself silver in the moonlight, and gazed down on the dead horse, "what are you doing here? Did you think to gain some of his strength and courage?" And she turned to look at her son and then back at Yarraman. "You should have it in your blood and bones already; he was, after all, your father. Use his courage and strength, son, and all the cunning and knowledge I have taught you. Come, we will leave him."

They jumped down and walked away together and at the mouth of the big valley she gave him a playful nip on the shoulder.

"I must get back to my foal. Good-bye!" but Thowra knew that their real "good-bye" had been said as they left the rock above the dead stallion.

Thowra went down the valley, left the cold, clear moonlight, crept through the trees, and back to Storm and the other colts.

At dawn they set off, towards the headwaters of the Crackenback River, a small mob of colts bound together only by habit and a common desire to put some distance between themselves and the dead stallion – their father – and to get away from possible trouble with The Brolga, who would now be the leader of the main sections of both herds.

Thowra had led off – really not bothering about any of the others following him except Storm, yet glad, in a way, of their company. However, even one day of travelling showed them that no mob can have two leaders, and Arrow, who had the size and strength to win any fight, would not peacefully let Thowra, the fastest and the one who knew the country best, become the acknowledged leader. He bit at Thowra and kicked him whenever they stopped to graze and drink, but when Thowra, tired of his behaviour, went off at the gallop with Storm, the other colts followed, so Arrow had to go too.

Thowra and Storm had often been in the Ramshead country since they were born there two years ago, and Mirri and Bel Bel had taught them all the good grazing places round the head of the Crackenback. They knew, too, where they could get up and down granite cliffs, where there were tunnels through what seemed impenetrable snowgum thickets, where there were deep holes in the creeks that a young horse could swim in, and easy crossing places in the rough-flowing river.

They led their young mob about, up on the high country among the snowdrifts, and right down in the great mountain ash gullies, where the lyre birds mimicked their neighing, or sent them galloping off in a frenzy by imitating the sound of a whip cracking or a man whistling.

After the first feeling of being left alone in a very large world had worn off, Thowra would have enjoyed everything if Arrow had not been such a bully. Arrow could not spoil it all because he could not go fast enough, but so often when they were grazing he would lash out savagely with his heels, or strike. Thowra was not afraid to fight him, though he always got the worst of it, but, except for Storm, the others would not take Arrow on, nor would they stay behind with him.

Once, Thowra, remembering the time when he had tricked Arrow and "lost" him, tried the same trick again. This time Arrow was missing for three days and he was much chastened when he joined them again.

It was then that Thowra began to think they should move over to Paddy Rush's Bogong because the men would be bringing their mobs of cattle again. He started off, early one morning, jogging down through the sun-glistening snowgums, through the mountain ash thickets and tangled woods of the little creeks, to the Crackenback, over it and up the rough country on the other side.

In the weeks that followed Thowra began to understand all his mother's warnings about Arrow making a bad enemy. The fights which Arrow forced on him were never half in fun, like most young colts' battles – an exuberance of strength and half-conscious wish to test and train themselves.

Arrow became more and more vindictive, and Thowra knew that his lovely silver mane hid some bite scars that he would carry to the end of his life. Also it became apparent that Arrow was trying to lame him, for Thowra, if lamed, could no longer be their half-acknowledged leader. Try though he did, Thowra could never worst Arrow in a fight, and, as the summer went on, Arrow became stronger and heavier, and more arrogant.

At last Thowra could stand him no longer.

"Let's go," he said to Storm, "next time there is a mist. Let's clear for the Brindle Bull country. Maybe The Brolga spends summer there, but if we keep away we'll come to no harm."

Two or three evenings later there were black clouds rolling up from the north and the following day came with rain and drifting cloud that hid everything. Thowra gave Storm a nip and, without waiting a moment, they melted quietly off.

There was a long, open glade of snowgrass up which they could canter, barely making a sound, then a little creek running over a sand and mica bed which they walked down, the water quickly filling in the tracks they made. While they were in the creek they heard a whinny through the cold mist, the thunder of hooves on stony ground, and then the crash of a rolling rock. The two colts drew right in under some blanket-woods that overhung the little stream and waited, breathlessly listening. They heard Arrow's imperious neigh, another rock falling, and the crack of a bough. Then the sound of hooves grew muffled in the cloud and Thowra and Storm went back up the stream and cut across country towards the Brindle Bull.

They were determined to stay on their own, now, and keep away from Arrow, and they were suddenly filled with excitement. They had never been on the mountain called the Brindle Bull and they would have a whole new world to explore. Even the touch of the cold, wet clouds, or the sting of a wet branch across the eyes, could not cool their excitement.

They did not stop except for an occasional drink, and they kept off any of the usual tracks in case, by any chance, the others had doubled back in the clouds. Finally they slithered down a smooth, wet rock face into the Crackenback River and stood, tired and trembling, while the water tugged at their legs.

By the time they were clambering up the steep, stony slopes of the Brindle Bull, the wet clouds had turned to rain, heavy, cold rain that felt as if it might become one of those swift flurries of snow in summer that leave the mountains gleaming white in a hot summer sky for a brief hour or two. It was hardly a good day for the start of an adventure, but the colts had been well taught by their mothers to find their way whatever the weather, and they kept on, scrambling up the steep slopes, pulling themselves up on rocky cliffs, forcing their way through shoulder-high heather till they were nearly at the top.

There they stopped where some snowgums grew thickly below a rock buttress, providing some shelter from the driving rain. As they stood there the clouds suddenly blew a few feet apart on the top of the mountain. Trembling with an excitement he did not understand, Thowra saw against the pale rift of sky, as though against a faintly lighted window, a herd of horses pass in ones and twos, like shadows — and they were led by a grey horse who seemed to melt into the clouds.

Chapter Ten

MAN ON A BLACK HORSE

THOWRA AND STORM were very careful where they went on the Brindle Bull, watching for tracks of The Brolga's herd, listening, smelling. It took them some days to find out the herd's grazing place, and after that they kept well away, down the sides of the mountain, in snowgum woods where there was only enough grass to make a picking for two colts.

There were one or two tiny hanging valleys on the southern slope, where the snow-daisies' leaves made a silver carpet and presently the daisies themselves, large and white, starred the ground. In one of these valleys the colts often grazed. There were rocky gorges off either side, and a quick getaway if they needed one.

The Brolga and his herd probably knew they were there, and were unworried by the presence of two young colts. Bel Bel may have recognized Thowra's spoor and been glad to know that he and Storm were close. Thowra being the only creamy foal she had borne, she had not forgotten him as a mare usually forgets a foal after it has become independent and left her. And because she often spoke of Thowra and Storm, Mirri remembered Storm, too.

One day the colts had wandered low enough to see into the Big Boggy Creek. Thowra had learnt now, in The Brolga's country, to use all the cunning Bel Bel had taught him and keep hidden in the fringe of trees, or in patches of light and shade. Often he had only just remembered in time to check his impulse to leap up on to a high rock before he had looked properly around first.

This time they peered into the valley of the Big Boggy from some hop scrub. There were a few cattle grazing along the grassy floor of the valley, the sight of which made them very cautious, but there was no sign of anything else. All seemed very peaceful, with no movement, other than that of the head-down cattle. Thowra leapt from one granite block to another till he was on top of a great heap of rocks. There was still nothing disquieting to see. Storm came up beside him.

"It is too open," said Thowra regretfully. "We would be foolish to go there, though some of that good grass would be nice."

They stood for quite a while, looking down longingly, and then moved slowly along the southern slopes, keeping the delicious-looking valley in sight. All of a sudden Thowra stopped and raised his head, his nostrils curling as he sniffed the air.

"Smoke!" He moved to a steep edge to see.

First he looked at the northern sky to judge if the wind had brought the smoke from a distant fire, then he looked closely into the valley. It was a second or so before he saw anything, then it was just a thin ribbon of smoke winding up through some snowgums, on the other side of the valley where a tiny creek came down. Just at that moment a man walked down the creek a few yards, and stopped to fill something with water.

"Man!" he hissed to Storm. "We must go before there is any chance of him seeing us."

They slid – one horse a dark shadow, one a piece of dappled, moving light and shade – through the scrub, heading towards their small hanging valley. And there, in the valley of the Big Boggy, drinking tea from his quart-pot, was a very young man who could think of nothing but the sight of a beautiful cream-coloured colt with flowing silver mane and tail, poised high above him on a heap of granite rock.

The two young horses made their way back to their camping-ground, and the young man, when he had finished his lunch, crossed the Big Boggy and started up the mountain towards the granite rock.

Thowra did not really think he had been seen, or he and Storm would have been far more worried, but he remembered how Bel Bel had shown him how to track other horses, and how not to leave tracks. Instinctively he chose snowgrass or rocks to walk on, wherever possible.

Thus it was that the young man tracked them easily from the granite rocks to the hop scrub, and then had the greatest difficulty in picking up their trail. He lost it so often that he gave up, as evening drew on, and lit his fire, boiled his quart-pot, and presently rolled up in the one blanket he had carried in front of his saddle, and went to sleep.

Thowra and Storm smelt the smoke from their hidden valley. Bel Bel and Mirri smelt the smoke, and The Brolga smelt it, too.

The man's little fire burnt all night long because it was a cold night and he, with only one blanket, kept waking and throwing on another log. His horse, picketed close to him, snuffled and stamped throughout the night.

It was only by luck – bad luck – that the man found Thowra's and Storm's hiding-place the next morning. He had failed to find their trail and just happened to ride out on to one of the few places that overlooked their hanging valley. There he sat on his tame black horse, the sleepy-looking, very young man, who suddenly became wide awake as he saw below him, on a carpet of snow-daisies, a good-looking bay colt and the supremely beautiful creamy.

The young man sat perfectly still, only his eyes moving as he looked at the valley, trying to find a way in, trying to see if there would also be a way out for the brumbies to take. Just then – and this was good luck – his horse whinnied.

Thowra, who for a moment or two had experienced a prickly feeling in his hair, knew instantly they were being watched. He threw up his head, the early sunlight like water on his rippling, lovely coat, and saw the man trying hastily to back out of sight.

As though caught in a willy-willy, Thowra whirled round and away, followed by Storm, into the clump of low snowgum and heather that hid the narrow opening into a gorge. But they heard, as they went, the crashing of rocks as the man came straight down the cliff on which he had been standing.

"If he gets down unhurt, he'll be after us, pretty close," Thowra thought, and strained his ears to hear what was happening behind. The crashing of rocks continued, purposeful crashing, as if someone kept forcing a horse down, not as if he had fallen and gone bouncing down among the boulders.

Thowra and Storm burst out of the scrub and up the rocky gorge. Suddenly Thowra turned right, leaping like a goat from rock to rock up the side of the gorge. He had noticed not long before that there might be a possible place of escape up this way, and now was certainly the time to use it. No ridden horse, he thought, would be able to follow.

He and Storm were blowing and sweating when they reached the top of the wall. They turned and looked down and saw the man already following. He leapt off his tame horse and started leading it up behind him. Thowra did not wait to see how he got on, but picked his way carefully over a great slope of wet and mossy rock.

"Keep off the moss, if you can," he warned Storm. "It will show our track. If we leave no track from the top of the cliff it will give us a few minutes extra." His feet slipped, then, with a grating clatter, and he went down on his side on the cold rock, but he leapt up and went on, then across some spongy, wet snowgrass, and into the cover of the trees.

There they stopped for a second and listened. There was

no sound. Off they went again, as fast as they could up the steep hill, trying not to set hoof on any soft, wet earth. Then, ringing out through the bush came the sound of a shod horse's hoof on a rock.

"He must be good, that tame horse," thought Thowra, but he did not guess that he was *extremely* good, nor that he had been fed on oats, and bran, and chaff, on which a horse can gallop much faster than on mountain grass, however sweet and lovely that grass may be.

Thowra began to feel frightened. They were near a great semicircle of rock cliffs that enclosed most evil-seeming bogs – the soft-surfaced, green bogs in which a horse could flounder and sink from sight, black mud bogs that were bottomless, and the squelching sphagnum bogs that no horse really trusted. But both he and Storm knew a track through all this, so, gasping for breath, he made straight for the lower arm of the cliffs.

Thowra stood on the rocks above the great hollow filled with bogs, and then took a flying leap on to a patch that he knew was solid ground. In a minute Storm was beside him – and had left no track to show where they had entered the hollow.

They could not go any faster than a walk, hearing all the time the squelch of water in sphagnum, feeling the awful, unstable surface under their hooves. Behind them, Thowra was sure he could hear a horse galloping. If he tried to go faster he kept imagining himself sinking in the great, treacherous mud holes. He looked up at the dark, water-stained cliff above him, and knew there was no escape there if the man caught up with them. He started to trot in terror, but nearly floundered into an innocent-looking green patch, and had to back out.

The other side was not far away, and they reached it before the man appeared. Ahead of them lay some wide, open country where they would have to gallop as fast as they possibly could. All of a sudden Thowra knew why he had come just this way. Sometimes The Brolga and his herd grazed here; and other wild brumbies – even the stallion that had killed Yarraman – would be better company than a lone man with a lasso. Also, perhaps, if there were numbers of horses, the man would not know which one to chase.

But there was no sign of any other brumbies; they must be in a higher grazing-ground still. With pounding hearts, the two colts galloped across the wide, open snowgrass, leaping the little streams, galloping with all their might for the trees and cover before the man saw them.

Thowra looked back over his shoulder once. There he came, sitting well down in the saddle, leaning forward over the powerful horse's neck. In that glance, Thowra realized that the tame horse was a four- or five-year-old, and therefore much stronger than he and Storm. He was desperate now, and could think only of reaching the herd.

The great black horse and its rider were gaining and gaining on them, even though they had a long start. Thowra and Storm stretched their legs even farther with each stride, and made tremendous efforts to go faster, faster. The trees were not far away. Thowra could see them through a red mist of exhaustion. The sunlight dancing on the leaves seemed like sparks or waves of light. He must reach that line of trees. He was done; he could not get his breath fast enough. Then he felt the vibration on the ground of the other horse drawing closer.

Hiss-s-s came the sound of the rope through the air.

Thowra shied violently at the sound, and the rope struck him a blow on the shoulder and then fell to the ground. Two more strides and the brumbies were in the trees.

The man would try to head them out into the open, Thowra knew, because he would not be able to rope them in the trees. Somehow they had to stay in timber till they reached the herd's next grazing-place. A flock of jays sent out warning cries, but the colts, with sweat streaming off them, did not hear.

Thowra realized they could hold their lead in timber, particularly if it was thick and low scrubby stuff. He was almost sure, now, that he was the one the man was after, and his terror drove him on ever faster. He knew this belt of timber went right to the top of the outside rim of a grassy basin. Perhaps the herd would be in the basin. The timber was thinner near the top and the man was gaining on him. Just as he reached the crest of the rim, he gave a wild, sobbing neigh for help. If the herd were not there it would be no use going into the open country, but they might be there. He paused for a second to look down, and saw the startled mob of brumbies below him. Once more he neighed, and then plunged down among them.

There were several shrill answering neighs, and an angry stallion roar, but the man came thundering down right beside him, taking no notice of the mob of brumbies.

Thowra knew that the black horse and rider were coming up almost alongside him now. Soon there would be the sound of the rope. Hiss-s-s! There it was! Again he leapt sideways. Again it struck him on the shoulder.

Then there were horses going everywhere, and Thowra was among them, legs stretching, stretching, breath sobbing... and someone was galloping shoulder to shoulder with him, pushing him to one side.

He was too tired, his eyes too blurred to see that it was a creamy mare, but even in his exhaustion he half realized that it was his mother, that somehow this had all happened before and he must just go where she took him. He did not see the leggy chestnut foal at her side.

Among the thunder of hooves and the wild galloping there was the different sound, quite close, of the shod horse, the jingle of his bit, the creak of his saddle. He had almost come up with them, and Thowra could go no faster, but he saw that there was some very thick scrub starting on their right and knew that Bel Bel must have somewhere to hide them and be going to wheel him into it. So he was ready for her when she swung him round and into a low tunnel of prickly scrub. There she pushed him round and into a low tunnel of prickly scrub. There she pushed ahead of him into the lead. For the first time he saw the leggy foal.

The scrub closed in behind them and they were suddenly surrounded in silence, though they could still hear the black horse crashing on over boulders.

Bel Bel led at quite a smart pace till she stopped abruptly

at the steep bank of a creek that flowed in a complete tunnel of wattle, blanket-woods and tree-fern. She jumped down into the water and turned upstream, only letting Thowra stop to drink for a moment, and then urging him on and on.

All sounds of other horses were getting very distant, but Bel Bel did not stop.

Thowra plodded after her up the stream, sometimes snatching a mouthful of the cold water, still panting, still trembling. He wondered where Storm had gone, but he knew he would be all right. It was he, Thowra, that the man on the black horse had been chasing.

The stream became very narrow and Thowra guessed they must be near the top of the mountain.

"Where we are going, we may find Mirri and Storm," Bel Bel said; but when they stopped in a little sandy cover that was completely hidden in scrub, there was no one there.

"They will come," she said again. "Lie down to rest." And when Thowra woke, hours later, Storm was asleep beside him.

Mirri and Bel Bel were standing looking at them while they placidly let their foals drink. Presently they led the two colts to a little field of snowgrass, and, as they themselves started back to the herd, Bel Bel said to her cream-coloured:

"Don't go back to where you were grazing. That man will remember you, and remember your haunts. Have you forgotten why I named you Thowra? I said then, at the time you were born, that every man would be after you, and you would have to be as fleet as the wind."

Brolga or Native Companion

Chapter Eleven

A TIME TO RACE WITH THE WIND

THOWRA AND STORM moved back on to the Main Range as soon as autumn began changing towards winter. For a while they stayed in the timbered country below the Ramshead, and often spent the lovely bright days galloping on the snowgrass between the granite tors. Sometimes there were other young horses near – and once Thowra was given quite a beating by a three-year-old stallion who came along with two or three young mares and seemed to want to fight him just because he looked different – but mostly they were on their own, and day after day was filled with a sort of wild joy as the weather grew colder and colder, and they galloped to keep warm, chasing sometimes a dingo, a hare, or a slinking red fox.

The snow was late that year, and in the clear autumn light the rocks looked purple, and the snowgums blended every red and orange and green with their ghostly silver grey. Thowra became lighter in colour as he got his winter coat, and, even more than in other winters, he looked silver rather than cream.

In the early mornings ice encased each blade of grass and leaf of heather along the little creeks; it crackled where the colts stepped. Often a glaze of ice on a shallow pool shivered and skidded away from their hooves. In the grass, the white frost brushed off on to their legs with every step. It was cold, so cold, but while the bright weather lasted, exciting and lovely, too.

Then came grey, bitter days with the north wind tearing over the mountains, when the young horses vied their speed with the wind's, galloping headlong down the springy grass towards the trees – and the trees were beating and lashing, like the wind-tossed mane on a wild horse.

At night they could hear the wind roaring in the mountains above them, or wailing and howling round the granite tors of the Ramshead Range. Sometimes it was hard to tell whether a dingo howled or whether it was just the wind between the rocks.

Thowra and Storm were becoming – as Brownie had said they would – lone wolves, like their two mothers.

Even the first flurry of snow did not drive them down lower – there was still grass to eat and a snowstorm to race through. Was there ever such a time as this, Thowra wondered, feeling his own strength as something that was his but yet part of the wind and the snow, and the great strength of the mountains. It was a time to gallop and a time to play; a time to race with the wind; a time to sleep below the rocks while the dingoes howled; a time for him and Storm to be alone in all their exciting strength – a time that was soon ending. With the spring would start a new period of the colts' lives, but between them and the spring lay this winter, and now the snow started to fall in earnest, and they were driven downwards for grass, at first as far as the headwaters of the Crackenback and the hut on the Gap called the Dead Horse Hut, and then on to the Cascades.

Thowra, though still terribly afraid of men, was also becoming very curious about them. If he found any old signs of them he could not keep away – as long as he knew the men had gone – and a hut seemed to him almost like magic. It was, after all, from these huts that their smoke came most often – and the fires that men lit were undoubtedly magic.

Dead Horse Hut had a roof of loose galvanized iron, and it creaked in the wind just as Storm was trying to persuade Thowra to walk past the hut without stopping to look all round it. Both colts leapt nervously back into the trees as they heard the sound and then, when it was repeated again and again as the cold wind streamed through the Gap, they crept forward once more. Nothing would now stop Thowra going carefully up to the hut to look and smell – and jump with fright each time the iron creaked. Storm stood in the trees, disapproving, until at last he realized that no harm was going to come to them and he too walked up cautiously, with nose outstretched. A very old saddle had been thrown down on the woodheap under the skillion roof. It smelt of horse, and they were bothered and backed away. Next they inspected the killing gallows which stood, like a windmill, stark against the snowladen sky. Near the gallows was a newly built stockyard with unusually high fences.

"If they catch any horses that will be where they put them. That's a yard, like Mirri used to tell us about," said Storm.

"You'd need to be able to jump," said Thowra, measuring the rails with his eye. "I could jump in, but I don't know whether I could get out."

"Don't try," said Storm. "The gate is tightly shut."

"You'd nearly get out at this lower corner, if you had to," Thowra said, but he turned around then, away from the hut. Storm gladly followed him up the next ridge, leaving the scents of man and tame horse behind them.

That night the black clouds massed up against the mountains and they knew that a really heavy snowstorm was coming. Instead of camping near good water and grass they kept jogging along towards the Cascades. They must get into lower country, but how many horses were wintering there at present, they did not know. Thowra felt he could beat Arrow now, if he had to fight him, but of course Arrow was not the only colt in the mountains.

By midnight snow was falling. They sheltered under some great rocks until the first grey streaks of dawn came, and then went cautiously downwards, keeping in among the trees.

They were right at the northern-most end of the Cascades – where the creek turned towards its great waterfall and the Indi River. This had been part of Yarraman's grazing-ground, and, in a valley which they avoided, his scattered, bleached bones might still be lying. The memory of that night, and the nearness to that place, made them nervous and very careful. Thus it was that they saw the group of horsemen, again led by that same splendid black horse, before they themselves were spotted. If they had kept going, they would have met head-on. As it was, Thowra and Storm stopped dead and tried to sneak off further into the timber; but once again that black horse neighed.

Quivering with fear, the two colts still crept as quietly as they could through the bush, but as soon as they heard the black horse and his rider following them, they broke into a wild gallop, heading for the roughest country they knew.

Soon they were tearing down a precipitous slope of big, loose boulders. This checked their pursuers, who dared not risk laming their horses.

Thowra and Storm watched them for a second, trying to get around below them. There were three others besides the man on the black horse, each one on a good, full-grown mount; each wearing a hat pulled down over his eyes, jodhpurs and leather coat that were soaked by falling snow.

As he stood for that one second, Thowra realized it was getting colder and the snow was falling more thickly. Perhaps it would turn into a real blizzard, and he would be blotted from sight – just fade into the atmosphere. But he would have to see he was not caught before there was enough snow on the ground and in the air to hide him. Then he thought of Storm – *his* colour would show up unless snow and mist and clouds really enfolded them both.

The men had got around below them, so Thowra began to climb steadily back on the loose, rolling boulders. He saw the horsemen split into two groups. It was time to make a dash for it across the boulders, over the timbered ridge, down on to the creek.

They had a good start on the men, and they went fast across the valley towards the forest near the Cascade hut. The snow fell cold on their steaming coats, thick-falling snow that was beginning to be hurtled, stinging, on the wind.

"We'll play hide-and-seek with them for a while, in the trees," Thowra said. "Then, if the snow gets heavier, you can dodge into the timber, and I'll make out into the open and lose them."

Snow was already starting to coat the leaves and fill the forks of trees. White rosettes were plastered by the wind against the jigsaw puzzle markings on the snowgum trunks. The ground was becoming white. It would not be long, Thowra knew, before he would be able to give his pursuers the slip… but he could hear them galloping. Then suddenly clouds of swirling snow began to fill the forest.

"It's almost thick enough, now," Storm said. "I'll go crashing off downwards, into the mountain ash, making enough noise for two, if you take to the open."

"Right," said Thowra. "Unless we're caught, we'll meet at the mouth of Yarraman's valley tonight."

Storm took off, thundering and crashing through the trees and the wild-blowing snow, breaking branches, kicking stones out behind him, giving a snorting neigh. Thowra stood dead quiet in a thick clump of tea-tree and hop scrub while the snowstorm grew densely white; then, he, too, gave a joyous neigh and set off for the open valley.

He didn't hear the man on the black horse swear and say, "That brumby is getting too cunning." But it was from that day on that a legend began to grow up about the cream brumby, cunning as a fox. Stockmen talked of him round their summer campfires, or sung songs about him as they rode around a restless mob of cattle at night, and the cattle told the brumbies, so that they too knew, all over the mountains, the tales of the wild cream brumby.

And Thowra? Thowra galloped down through the trees into the Cascades Valley, felt the good, springy snowgrass under the snow, listened to make sure that he was being followed, neighed again in bold triumph and set off as fast as he could go. He led them just the sort of dance he had often led Arrow, leaping creeks where they were narrow, hoping they would blunder in, skirting round deep holes that might throw them, tearing out on to rocky promontories and jumping off where he knew he had a good landing-place – and neighing if he thought the blizzard had got so thick that they might lose him.

Sometimes he looked back and could just make out the four other horses and their riders, like shadows, galloping, galloping, through the snow.

When he started to get tired, he turned back and quietly let the driving curtain of snow hide him from their sight.

The men had followed at first the crashing, dashing bay – that they did not want to catch. Then they had chased a mocking ghost that sometimes showed up as a pale, galloping outline in the snow-filled air, sometimes as a rearing, playing colt on a rock, but was, most often, only the sound of a neigh that echoed through the storm. Now they found themselves in the silence of the snowstorm, with only the distant rush and roar of the blizzard in the trees or round the rocky ridges. There was no sign nor sound of the cream brumby colt.

Thowra heard their voices getting smaller and more distant as they rode back towards the track to Groggin. He had found himself shelter in a few trees up a side valley, and, as the day wore on, he went back to meet Storm.

Koala Bear

Chapter Twelve

THE COMING OF SPRING

SPRING COMES TO the Australian Alps like an invisible spirit. There is not the tremendous surge of upthrust life that there is in the lowland valleys, and no wild flowers bloom in the snow mountains till the early summer, but there is an immense stirring of excitement. A bright red and blue lowrie flits through the trees; snow thaws, and the streams become full of foaming water; the grey, flattened grass grows upwards again and becomes greener; wild horses start to lose their winter coats and find new energy; wombats sit, round and fat, blinking in the evening sunshine; at night there is the cry of a dingo to its mate.

Thowra and Storm greeted the first warm, scent-laden breeze off the wattle on the foothills by wandering up towards the Ramshead, where the snow still lay. They were deeply restless and they soon came back nearer the

Cascades, where they found that in the few days they had been away other young colts had appeared, and that the fillies, among them some of the grey daughters of The Brolga, were galloping skittishly about away from the herd.

Thowra and Storm skirted round on the ridges above the main valley, watching.

They had had a rough winter, in a way, finding the other colts unfriendly and against them for being lone wolves. Thowra and Arrow had had only one fight and Arrow could still win, but in snowy weather Thowra had managed to be the invisible gadfly leading them all into trouble, even once daring to dash right through The Brolga's herd.

The Brolga was still very much king of the Cascade brumbies, but now it was clear that he was taking no notice of the young colts and fillies, just lording it over his own herd in the valley below.

Filled with restlessness and a longing for the company of the other young horses, Thowra and Storm went down a ridge to where there was a little group of fillies chasing each other in the sunshine.

Down they went to join in the play and found, to their surprise, that the fillies were just as likely to bite or kick them as to play. But before long Thowra realized they were pleased that he and Storm had joined them, even if they did put up a show of driving them off. So they galloped with them all that day; it was not until evening that they found themselves anywhere near other horses, and that was by mistake.

Thowra simply had not realized that The Brolga's herd was so near. When he saw them, he could not go away, for there, among the herd, were two more grey fillies like one they had been galloping with, and Thowra, suddenly knowing that he must gather together a herd of his own, decided that in it there must be the grey daughters of The Brolga.

In the heady springtime feeling of super strength, this did not seem in any way a silly thing to decide — not even when he saw Arrow standing with a few fillies behind him, some distance off, on a little hill.

Thowra noticed that The Brolga himself was not near the two grey fillies, so he squealed and started rearing and prancing in the broad band of an oblique evening sun ray that came between two shoulders of hill, his long mane and tail streaming, streaming, like silver pennons.

The two grey fillies neighed in answer and came cantering across. The Brolga turned and stared, lifted his head and roared angrily, then came trotting towards Thowra.

"Clear out quick," said Storm. "The fillies will come."

Thowra watched only long enough to see the two fillies coming close to them before he cantered away. The Brolga made a swift sally at them all, driving colts and fillies in front of him, roared his annoyance, and then turned back to his own herd, stopping every so often to look back, roar, and paw the ground.

Thowra and Storm cantered on with six fillies, the three greys, two browns, and a bay. They went steadily on, heading for the upland country. They did not see Arrow looking after them and then following with his own herd —

one golden chestnut colt with four fillies stringing along behind him.

Arrow had grown into a very handsome colt, still like his father, but his eyes showed their whites, and there was a mean, pinched look about his head, just as there was about Brownie's. The other colts were all afraid of him, not so much because he was far stronger, and a cunning fighter besides, but because of his meanness. He would be friendly with a horse for a while and then turn on him viciously, and all the young colts with whom he had been running had scars and blemishes on them from his kicks and bites.

Thowra was not afraid of him, but he knew that Arrow would try to maim him if he got a chance. Perhaps at the back of his head he knew that Arrow would sooner or later want to kill him, and he knew it was better to keep away.

Storm hated Arrow, but Storm, too, could gallop faster and farther and knew every yard of the country better than the big chestnut did. He knew instinctively that there would be trouble sometime, too, because he could see that Thowra had become so proud and beautiful as he grew up, and the other horse was beautiful too. Though the mountains were vast and wide, Arrow and Thowra might find there was not room for them both as they grew into mature stallions.

But neither Storm nor Thowra were thinking of Arrow now. They went on upwards, feeling proud and bold, stepping lightly on the springy tussocks of snowgrass.

Sunset turned every ridge and hill-top into molten gold, and the valleys below them into long fingers of blue shadow. They stopped to drink at cold, rushing streams, shying away from the floating foam, but the instinct to get further away from the great, grey Brolga kept them moving on till all the light had gone from the hills.

They camped that night in a little grove of snowgums that shielded them from the sneaking cold breeze. Arrow and his herd had not travelled so late into the evening, so they were quite a long way off.

There was still snow below the Ramshead, so Thowra only went as far as the lovely open fields of snowgrass on The Ridge above the Dead Horse Gap. It was here, at midday, that Arrow caught up with them.

Heedless, and filled with an unbounded pride in his own strength and beauty, Arrow came trotting out of the trees towards the two grey fillies whom he had been admiring in The Brolga's herd. His golden mane rippled as he tossed his head: he carried his tail high. All the sunlight seemed to concentrate on the glittering, golden colt.

The fillies knew he was there before Thowra and Storm did, and watched, fascinated and afraid. Then both the colts saw him at once, and, both roaring with rage, galloped towards him, their teeth bared.

Arrow had never seen Storm enraged before and had not expected him to rush into the attack too. He turned and galloped away with the screaming, angry colts driving him back to his own fillies. The fillies fled too. Storm and Thowra drove the whole little herd away towards the Cascades, then feeling very pleased with themselves they returned to their group of waiting fillies.

★　★　★

It was three years now since Bel Bel and Mirri had nodded their heads wisely over their two foals, knowing they would be mates, knowing they would fulfil the way of the brumbies and run as colts together after they had left their mothers and until they had to fight for a herd of their own. Now had come the time when each one wished to take his herd off on his own, so Storm, with his browns and bay, and Thowra, with his grey fillies, drifted apart, grazing in different directions every day, till each young stallion was let alone with his own mares.

They had weeks, yet, before the cattle mobs – and the men – would come to the mountains, and this year the snow was lying late on the main tops. Thowra, with his love of the high, rocky places, often took his mares right up between the Ramsheads, where there were great drifts of snow in which to roll, and they might spend days grazing on the sweet upland grass. It was most unlikely that any enemies would be there to worry him, and he did not feel he had to take his usual care to keep hidden. The lovely bright days were spent roaming in the sunshine, leaping from rock to rock up in the tors, galloping down the long grass slopes or the lanes between the different Ramsheads. But one day Arrow came.

Arrow was not adventurous, and ordinarily nothing would have made him go alone with his mares into the higher mountains, but he was in a jealous fury with Thowra for having taken the grey fillies.

He came in the morning, quite early, and Thowra and his mares were all four standing up in the bright sunlight on the slabs of a tor, the spring breeze gently lifting their manes, when they saw Arrow below.

Thowra was just going to fly down and chase him but he remembered that this time Storm was not there, and Arrow would fight.

"He can come up here," he thought, and looked around for the best position. He put the mares behind him, with unclimbable cliffs around them, and then stood facing Arrow.

Arrow did not even stop to think that his superior strength would not be much advantage from below: he came leaping and prancing up the rocks, completely confident of himself – only to get a deadly blow on the head from Thowra's forefoot as he came within striking distance.

He was knocked back and downwards, and was very shaken. He could feel blood trickling between his eyes, but he still did not imagine that he could be beaten. He came up again, angrily – and received the same treatment. This time he stopped to think, realizing that he could hardly expect anything else, with Thowra in such an impregnable position above him. He decided then that if he waited, just below, where there was a pool of water from which he could drink, Thowra and his mares would have to come down some time; on level ground he could easily win a fight. So he had a drink and then stood and waited in the shade of a rock, while the sun beat down on the four that were on the tor.

It did not take Thowra long to see through his plan, and he could only hope that Arrow would get tired of waiting, but after an hour or so had gone by, he began to get thirsty. Arrow seemed to be making a great show of drinking at the little pool.

"Trust him to be mean-spirited if he could be," thought Thowra bitterly. Then in a fury he decided it was better to go down and fight before he got too thirsty and too stiff from standing on the rocks. At least he would have the advantage of a downhill gallop, straight at Arrow, but he must not go too fast or Arrow would easily sidestep him.

Telling the mares to stay where they were, Thowra sprang lightly down from rock to rock, muscles rippling under his gleaming cream coat, eyes keen, nostrils quivering, ears pricked.

Arrow strutted out into the open to meet him, but Thowra could see he was alert, ready to dodge to one side. Thowra started to gallop straight for him, but slackened speed just a little as he drew close – knowing that he was much more nimble on his feet than Arrow.

Arrow leapt aside, but Thowra swung round, pivoting magnificently on his quarters, and struck him furiously with his forelegs. He saw blood spurt again above Arrow's eyes, but then Arrow was coming for him with open mouth and his lips drawn back. Thowra jumped and struck again, and leapt forward too, to try to get first hold on Arrow's wither. He had him for a short time, but his hold was not good enough, and Arrow fought free.

Thowra knew his only chance of success lay in his quickness, so he danced round Arrow, darting in with a strike, a bite, or a kick – dancing, dancing, rearing, plunging, pivoting, swinging round like a flash. The effort was tremendous, and he was very thirsty, but he could see that the pace was tiring the heavier horse. Sweat was turning Arrow's coat dark, and Thowra could hear his heavy breathing.

On and on they fought, the grass churned to mud underfoot, the smell of blood and sweat all round them, and the sun beating down, then sinking so that its rays sometimes blinded them.

Thowra occasionally saw that same red film of exhaustion in front of his eyes that he remembered when he had had to gallop for his life from the man on the black horse, but he knew Arrow must be even more exhausted because he was making more and more desperate efforts to get a hold or to place a solid strike, so he kept on dancing, and plunging, and pivoting, trying to wear him out as quickly as he could.

There were great bites on Thowra's withers, and he had a gash over one shoulder from a vicious strike – if he kept moving *that* wouldn't stiffen – but he was tired, so tired, aching in the legs, in the shoulders, in the quarters. His heart was pounding, and he could hear his own breath sobbing now, but Arrow's breathing was louder still.

And so they fought until they were both completely exhausted, and neither could beat the other. Arrow had certainly given Thowra more serious wounds, but Arrow was unable to fight any more. When he backed off, Thowra followed him, trying to make a pretence of driving him, but he was too tired even to bite.

Arrow went, and Thowra dropped his nose into the pool of water and drank and drank. Presently there was a soft whinnying from the mares who came to drink too and to be with their young stallion. And as the sun sank below the mountains, the light faded and died. Slowly the stars came into the sky, and soon, the deep blue darkness above the mountains and the horses, the Southern Cross burned.

Thowra lay on the grass beside the stream, too aching and stiff and tired to move.

Kurrawong—Australian Magpie or Piping Crow

Chapter Thirteen

LEGENDS OF THOWRA

MEN WITH PACK-HORSES, stocking up the huts, came earlier than the mobs of cattle that year. They were there, at Dead Horse Hut, before the brumbies got any warning, and Thowra, grazing with his mares on some open snowgrass about half a mile away, knew he had been seen.

He melted backwards into the forest, but it was time to go from the Main Range, and, without waiting a moment, he took his mares with him and set off for the Brindle Bull. In the evening, they crossed the full-foaming river, fighting through the current, and the red stain of the sunset on the water reminded Thowra of the blood that had run from his wounds into the creek after his fight with Arrow. He wondered where Arrow would spend the summer, and thought probably on Paddy Rush's Bogong, and that there would be more chance of keeping his little herd on the

Brindle Bull, where The Brolga grazed, than too close to Arrow.

Instinctively, when they climbed the mountain the next day, he led his herd towards the hanging valley on the south slope. They would be safe there for a little while. The man with the black horse would more likely look for them at the Cascades in the early summer. Also he knew that if Storm were coming he might come there too. And one bright evening, when the kurrawongs were calling and the grey, red-crested gang-gangs chattering in the trees, Storm came down their track, and the two young stallions trotted up to greet each other, whinnying softly.

"Brothers of the wind are we," Thowra said, as they nipped each other playfully. "It is good that we should be together again," and for all that summer and the crisp autumn, and during the winter with its snow and cold winds, and while their young mares were getting heavier with foal, the two stallions and their herds ran together.

Neither the summer nor the autumn were quiet. There seemed often to be men about. The man on the black horse chased them several times, but all the cunning that Bel Bel had taught Thowra, and his ever-increasing speed, kept him safe. Twice Storm took the two herds away and left the men galloping after Thowra so that Thowra had more chance of vanishing down a tunnel of scrub or into a deep hole in a stream. But it was never so easy to escape if the men had dogs.

Round the campfires the legends of the cream brumby – his speed, his cunning, his extraordinary beauty – grew and grew. The cattle heard them in the soft starlight nights, and gradually Bel Bel, running with The Brolga, heard these tales and was pleased and afraid, all at the same time. There was one foal she had had that she would never forget.

Some of the stories that were woven round Thowra were strange stories, too. There was one that Bel Bel heard of how some men were sleeping in the open round a campfire one night, and of how one of the company had woken with the feeling of being watched. Then, in the trees, he had seen a pale stallion vanishing from sight. There was another tale of two men and their pack-horses, and of how they had observed a wraithlike horse appear and disappear in the bush beside their track, keeping pace with them for several miles. All this worried Bel Bel. She kept saying to Mirri that the tales they heard could not be true, but she wondered.

They were true, of course. Thowra was so curious! However, more than once he had saved the two small herds from being hunted by knowing where the men were and which way they were going. As his strength and his speed increased he could not help enjoying the excitement and danger of watching the men and their horses, and of pitting his cunning against them. He knew that one of the legends about him was that he had never left a hoofmark by which he could be traced. He knew, too, that many of the stockmen did not believe he really existed. This much he heard from the grazing red and white cattle, or from the single beasts he met in the river pools.

As the months went by he even felt less anxiety about Arrow, forgetting that Arrow, also, would be growing in strength with each passing day. They did not see each other until the winter, neither having sought the other out. It did not suit Arrow to fight without winning, but his summer and autumn had been less troubled by stockmen – every man in the mountains, whether they believed in the silver stallion's existence or not being out to catch Thowra – and Arrow had come to regard himself as invincible. However, when the two stallions saw each other in the distance, there was no real reason to fight – there was food enough for all, and springtime was the time to fight for mares – so they went on their separate ways.

The winter's storms came then, and in the whirling, swirling snow Thowra and his herd of three grey mares were often invisible, often able to play tricks on the others, and enjoy the wild games.

So Thowra's first year with a herd of his own passed very happily, and he felt within himself the mounting tide of energy and joy which even the intense cold and the great storms could not quench. Then when the first warm, scent-laden winds came, and the warm rains to wash away the thawing snow, Thowra's strength rose with the streams, grew with the grass and the buds and leaves.

All the mountains, the silent, rolling, grey-green hills, the great rock cliffs and crags, the rushing streams, and the dense forests, were his kingdom, possessed, because of his joy, his speed, his strength and his beauty, possessed perhaps even more than Arrow possessed them, or The Brolga – possessed, really, because of what Bel Bel had given him, the wanderlust and the understanding of every sign of bird and beast and weather.

Spring was coming to all this mountain kingdom. Foals would be born, young kangaroos, possums, and wombats would be snugly in their mothers' pouches, the hawks and great wedge-tail eagles would hatch their young, fat dingo pups would roll in the sunshine, and the wild horses would fight for their mares and gallop over the hills in all the glory of their strength.

Wallaby and her young

Chapter Fourteen

SWIFT ARROW

BEL BEL LISTENED to the trumpeting spring calls of the stallions that were in and around the valley of the Cascades. First she heard Arrow's call, followed by The Brolga's ringing answer, and now with a challenge in its sound. Then she heard Thowra's call, and knew undoubtedly it was his.

All the love of the high, wild places, all the amazing joy in being alive sounded in his voice.

Bel Bel, who was growing old, knew that she would indeed live on in her cream son, and she could imagine him standing high above the valley on a rocky promontory, the sunlight on his shining cream coat and on the streaming silver of his mane and tail, calling out for joy.

When she heard Arrow's call again it sounded closer to Thowra. Bel Bel started moving in the same direction, with a sudden sense of foreboding. Then she heard her son again, and a clangour of echoes, and knew he must be moving up a narrow valley. She started climbing up a ridge, lithely and swiftly, in spite of her age.

Again she heard Arrow, shriller and more urgent, and by the faint echo, she knew he was entering the valley. This time Thowra definitely answered him in a ringing challenge; and now Thowra had risen out of the valley because the sound of his challenge rang out over the hills.

Bel Bel started to move faster. She knew the ridge she was on rose to quite a high knob then dropped and climbed again. From the knob she would have a commanding view.

Had the time come when the vast mountains were no longer vast enough for two such stallions as Arrow and Thowra? Arrow, Bel Bel knew, had only become more jealous and mean-spirited as he grew up. He had wanted Thowra's grey mares badly enough last year. This year he had probably made up his mind to get them.

Often, as she climbed, she heard their trumpeting, challenging cries.

Round some rocks she came face to face with a dingo: both she and the yellow dog jumped nervously, and went on their way.

A roaring challenge from Arrow echoed and echoed round the narrow valley, but from far above came the mocking answer, as though Thowra was laughing there in the sun.

Bel Bel was not laughing, though. She had seen Arrow often lately and noticed that he was an almost mature horse, heavy and strong, so like his father, Yarraman, in all except temperament. And Thowra, Thowra was much more her son than Yarraman's, fleet of foot, like she was, and lithe. In this fight, now, he would be fighting for his life.

Up and up, Bel Bel climbed, hearing all the time the wild stallion calls that grew fiercer and more insistent. At last, she reached the top of the knob and stood there scanning the surrounding country. Far away, she could see Thowra and his mares, but Arrow was not yet in sight. She waited and watched. Between her and Thowra there was a stretch of very rough bush country with some great heaps of granite rocks and one or two high cliff faces, but opposite, where Thowra was, there were open fields of snowgrass.

As she watched she saw the three mares disappear from sight into the bush and then saw Thowra rear on his hind legs, almost as though dancing with joy; then he screamed his defiance. Arrow was coming up out of the valley into view!

The big chestnut came slowly, stopping now and then to paw the ground in anger and anticipation.

Bel Bel held her breath. What was Thowra going to do? She thought she knew: she *hoped* she knew.

Arrow's mares were in sight now; and Arrow was advancing slowly, his screams becoming shriller and shriller. Bel Bel, even from that distance, could almost sense his quivering fury. It would have taken a better-tempered horse than Arrow to remain calm against Thowra's taunting. The creamy danced and mocked with a rudeness unbelievable, but his movements were quiet and rhythmical, taking none of the energy he would soon need.

Arrow stopped and pawed the ground, then came on again, rearing, snorting, screaming.

Thowra roared a mocking challenge in reply; waited till Arrow got quite close, and then pirouetted and galloped on to some rocks a hundred yards away.

Bel Bel heaved a sigh.

Arrow broke into a gallop and followed, obviously trusting to the impetus of his rush to knock Thowra clean off the rocks. Thowra danced to one side, swung round, and struck him a drumming kick in the ribs, one calculated to infuriate more than to damage, and Arrow went flying down the other side of the rocks, pulled up on his haunches, and came back at him.

Thowra waited a moment and then leapt down and away to another vantage point. This time it was only a grassy hillock and he did not let Arrow get close enough to strike or bite him, but, giving a derisive roar, galloped back to the heap of rocks.

Bel Bel saw that he was doing everything to goad Arrow to anger. It was a long time since she had watched Thowra really move, and it was clear that because of his speed he had all the advantages if he did not let Arrow really come to grips with him. But if it came to a ding-dong fight, there was no question about it: she was sure Arrow would win.

Thowra remained just sufficiently out of Arrow's reach to keep the bigger horse at a wild pitch of anger, and Bel Bel watched him leading the way slowly nearer the bush. Once they were among the trees, she would not be able to see how the battle went.

The sweat was breaking out on her already, trickling from behind her ears. Thowra *must* win, and yet she did not really know how. Supposing Arrow killed him — her beautiful cream foal to whom she had taught everything she knew of the bush!

She saw Thowra gallop through the first of the trees with Arrow close behind. Then there were just flashes of colour as they dodged among the snowgums, and Arrow's scream rang out shriller and angrier while Thowra mocked him more and more, until it seemed almost as if the cream and silver brumby were laughing aloud.

Then Bel Bel held her breath again. Through the trees it looked as if Arrow had caught Thowra, and was trying to get the first fatal hold above the wither; but she was mistaken. There was Thowra streaking between the trees; there was his derisive cry again, mocking Arrow. For one minute she could see him prancing in a little clearing. He was closer to her now, and it was not just in imagination and memory that she saw his beauty.

For a little longer she watched him galloping down a glade, then they both vanished, and she could only hear the screams, both furious and mocking.

All of a sudden Thowra burst into view, galloping straight for the top of one of the cliffs, Arrow fast on his heels.

Bel Bel stood tense and still.

Thowra checked on the very edge, stones flying in the air, and then, just as Bel Bel had jumped with him years before, over another cliff, he jumped on to a tiny ledge quite some feet below the top. There he stopped, rocking unsteadily for a moment. Bel Bel saw him look up to see what Arrow was doing. And Arrow? Flying through space, carried far out from the cliff face by his speed, was Arrow.

To Bel Bel it seemed ages of time before Arrow crashed on to the ground at the foot of the cliff; until he stopped hurtling through the air; until he crashed and lay absolutely still.

Bel Bel only stayed long enough to see Thowra step carefully along the wallaby track round the cliff from his narrow shelf, and then she set off towards him at a trot. But Thowra had not seen her and she soon saw that he was going to head back to his mares. Bel Bel kept on. She wanted to see what had happened to Arrow. She saw Thowra glance back over his shoulder often, and realized then that he had not been able to see Arrow's crash from his ledge, and that now he was determined to get back to his mares before Arrow could find them. She kept on towards the bottom of the cliff.

She crossed a bush-filled hollow and drank at a little stream. A brown wallaby sat gravely watching her, and some gang-gangs threw gum-nuts from the trees.

She went on, looking for Arrow. Suddenly she stopped. Somewhere she seemed to have seen the same thing before — a chestnut stallion lying in a crushed and huddled heap, with all the tremendous life completely gone from him. In among the shaley rocks at the foot of the cliff, Arrow lay dead.

Thowra had fought for his life using his own weapon — his speed. He had planned his escape, not Arrow's death — but Arrow was as dead as Yarraman had been when the mountains were no longer vast enough to hold him and The Brolga.

She stood looking at Arrow. His head, the only part of him which revealed his mean spirit, was doubled and underneath his neck and the golden mane flowed over it. Already a crow had arrived, and was advancing on the dead horse with little hops. A flight of lowries, scarlet and royal blue, flew through the trees, heeding neither Bel Bel nor Arrow. Over the rocks moved a little brown lizard.

Bel Bel shuddered and backed away slowly to start on the steep climb round the cliff.

The bush seemed very silent now, after the noise of the two stallions. She began to doubt if she would find Thowra. As he did not know that Arrow was dead, he was certain to take his mares and go right away. Anyway, she would try to find him. But when she got to the top she could not go on without once again going to the cliff edge and taking a last look – perhaps to make sure that Arrow, who had harried her foal from his first day with the herd, was really dead.

She stood on the grey granite edge and looked over. There was the heap of chestnut and gold, and she forgot for a moment that it was Brownie's son. With his narrower, pinched head not showing, he looked the image of Yarraman.

A sound came from behind her! She turned in a flash. There was Thowra coming out of the bush.

"Everything was so quiet," he said. "I had to come and see what had happened."

"He could not stop," said Bel Bel. "He's down there, dead."

Thowra peered over the edge, his sweat-stained ears twitching nervously.

"Come away," Bel Bel said, backing. "It is too open here. You must go back to your mares – and Arrow's if you want them."

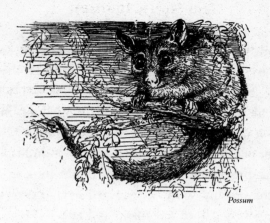

Possum

Chapter Fifteen

GOLDEN THE BEAUTIFUL

THOWRA DID NOT forget that the men had come early last spring, so even when the long fingers of snowdrifts still stretched down the southern slopes and deep snow lay in the gullies, he kept a careful lookout.

He was both proud and embarrassed by the size of his herd now. Besides a rather handsome black mare of Arrow's that he had added to his greys, there were two strange-looking little dun-coloured foals, Arrow's chestnut daughter, and one creamy colt. He did not take much notice of the foals, but he realized that they made his herd slower and less easy to hide.

For a week or more they had been grazing near the headwaters of the Crackenback and Groggin Gap, when one evening, quite late, Thowra heard sounds in the bush, first the jangle of a bit, and then the *frou-frou-frou* rub of packs on tree-trunks.

He and his herd were not on the stock track, so, telling his mares to stay still, he slipped silently through the already darkening bush, closer and closer to the sounds. Then suddenly he stood absolutely still. Walking along the track, her rider leading one pack-horse, was a cream filly. There were other pack-horses and one stock horse and rider at the end of the procession, but Thowra could look at nothing else but the creamy, with her proud carriage and swinging stride, the lovely silk of her mane and tail.

For a while, he moved silently through the trees parallel with the track, watching and watching her.

The men seemed to be tired out and swaying, half-asleep in their saddles. They did not even hear her whinnying softly when she looked through the bush and saw Thowra.

Thowra knew quite well that the men must be going to the Dead Horse Hut, their pack-horses loaded with stores of tinned foods, and flour, and salt for the cattle. He turned back to his herd to put them in a safe place for the night, knowing that he must return to the hut himself. A half moon came up a few hours later, enough to see by and yet not so light that Thowra could not keep himself well hidden.

Before going very near the hut, he walked along the horse-paddock fence. He could see the pack-horses, moving like restless shadows, but there was no sign of the two riding-horses, neither the creamy nor the other whose colour he had not even noticed. He had rather expected that they would be left in that new yard whose high fences he and Storm had studied more than a year ago.

The timber was cleared quite a long way back from the yard, which stood out on its own against the horse-paddock fence, in front of the hut.

Thowra moved through the trees very slowly, seeking the dark pools of shadow and avoiding any glades where the moonlight shone. A possum watched him with its wistful yet curious, pointed face. It gave a deep, throaty qua–a–r–rk, and he heard the sound of horses shuffling in the yard. He stood at the edge of the trees looking across. Yes, there, silvered by moonlight, was the lovely filly. She whinnied softly again, and a man opened the hut door, the light from a hurricane lamp blending with the moonlight.

A voice said, "The brumbies might be about." And another voice inside the hut answered: "Don't worry. The fence is mighty high, but you was a fool to bring her, all the same." Then they shut the door again and soon the hurricane lamp was turned out.

After waiting a long time, Thowra walked across the open ground to the yard. The cream filly came up to the fence, trembling with excitement, and put her nose through to snuff him.

As she started to whinny he said:

"No. No. You must learn to be silent, if you would come with me. What is your name?"

"They call me Golden. You must be Thowra of whom all the other horses speak – and the men even have songs about you that they sing to the cattle, but *they* call you Silver."

"Thowra is my name," said Thowra proudly. "The name my mother, Bel Bel, gave me."

Just then the bay stock horse, who had been standing trembling in the yard, let out a shrill, ringing neigh. Thowra was gone in a flash, silent-footed but fast, back into the bush. He was barely hidden in the trees before he heard the hut door opening and saw a man come out with a torch. Thowra watched him go right over to the yard, where the horse and the cream filly stood snorting, and turn his torch on to the ground. When he heard him say, "Huh, an unshod horse!" Thowra knew it was time to go, and to go on rocks and grass where he left no track.

Last year the men who had brought the pack-horses out early had stayed two nights. These men would probably too – but would they perhaps hobble the horses the next night, or watch over them in turns, hoping to catch him? He decided to wait till later in the night and then go back.

The moon had gone behind a bank of cloud when Thowra next stood on the edge of the bush and peered through the leathery snowgum leaves towards the yard. He could see Golden moving restlessly about, but the other horse seemed to be asleep.

Stepping from one snowgrass tussock to another, he moved towards the yard again, this time making for the only place in the fence where there was grass and not bare earth.

Golden came up to him again.

"How high can you jump?" Thowra asked her. "There is one lower place in this fence over there in the corner."

"I'd never clear that," said Golden.

"Not even if I jumped in and gave you a lead out over it?" But he eyed the bay horse. With that silly jackass there to bray, the game would be given away before they could get out.

Just then the bay horse stirred; he threw up his head with a startled snort, and then neighed loudly.

"Jump, and come with me," Thowra said, as he turned to go. Already there was a clatter in the hut and a man's voice cursing.

Thowra bounded away over the grass. He looked back, but Golden was not following, and before he had quite reached the trees he heard the door open. He was hidden by the time the man appeared but it had been a near thing. Thowra watched the man prowling around, saw that he could find no more tracks and that he was puzzled. Presently he went back inside, but there were still sounds of him moving about, and then came the smell of smoke as it poured through the hut chimney.

Just then the dawn wind came, stirring the darkness of the night, touching with cool long fingers Thowra's coat, his ears; whispering through the snowgum leaves. Daylight would soon come, and he must not be seen, but he could not tear himself away and he remained, never taking his eyes off the yard. The man came out with a pannikin of tea in his hand and leant on the yard fence. He called Golden. To Thowra's amazement he saw her walk over to him and take something out of his hand and eat it.

Thowra tossed his head and turned away into the thick bush. He made no sound as he went back to his herd, but Golden's whinny followed him. He stopped for a second and listened, not understanding how she could whinny to him and yet accept something from the man. But the whinny sealed his determination to get her for himself.

The presence of his own herd made it awkward. He realized that fully when he came through the trees and found them in a glade that was filled with the liquid gold of early morning sunshine. They looked beautiful, his greys with their tiny odd-coloured foals, and the one lovely cream one. He must not take the chance of being chased by the men himself, and his herd being found — but how wonderful it would be to have Golden there with the greys.

That morning he led the herd up towards the Ramshead, and put them in a gully that opened to the north-west and was bare of snow. Then he turned back to the hut, going carefully and quietly through the thickest bush, and leaving hardly a hoofmark.

All his senses were alert. He heard the faintest rustle made by an early-moving snake, saw its beady eye. He felt, before he saw, the gang-gangs looking at him, their red crests up. When two kangaroos went hopping by rather quickly he went more carefully still. Then, in the distance, he heard the sound of a shod horse. Thowra slid farther into the thick scrub, and stood waiting.

Presently he heard two horses approaching, and when he knew they had passed, he drew closer. There were the two men riding Golden and the bay horse. The packs must have been left behind, which meant the men would stay another night. He followed for a while to see what they were doing. They were wandering without direction, looking for something – and, if it were his tracks they were looking for, they were wasting their time, because they were not going to find any.

He turned back to the hut and had a look around. The packhorses were grazing in the horse paddock. Everything was as he thought. He headed for the Ramshead and the herd.

That night Thowra went to the hut again, stepping proudly through the dark forest before the moon had risen. Leaves brushed his shoulders and there was the lovely damp scent of the bush at night. He kept thinking of what Bel Bel would say to such a foolhardy expedition as this – and yet he knew she would understand. She was creamy herself and could appreciate how lovely the cream filly was. It was Storm who would really consider him a fool.

He kept watch for a long time from the edge of the trees, slightly surprised that Golden showed no sign of knowing he was there, but he had been even more silent than before, and Golden's senses were not as sharp as a wild horse's.

The fire and the lamp were both out in the hut, and all was quiet. He could see no man watching over the horses, and the horses were not hobbled. Still suspecting a trap, he came out of the trees slowly, thankful that the moon had not yet risen. He reached the fence, his skin pricking with nervousness, but nothing happened. The bay was sound asleep.

He measured up the fence again, and in the springtime surge of strength and spirits, he felt sure that he would be able to jump out and lead Golden away.

He backed off, speeded up as quietly as he could, and jumped.

"Now, come on and follow me!" he said to Golden.

The bay woke with a startled squeal. A man burst out of the hut, shouting:

"Got you, my beauty!"

"Come quick!" said Thowra, and with only the very short run available in the yard, he took three strides and made a prodigious leap. His knees rapped the top rail, yet he still seemed to lift higher. A rope whistled and fell short. Thowra felt his heart almost bursting with fear and effort, but he was over! The other man was running with a rope, too.

Thowra swung wildly and felt it hit his flank. Golden called, but she was still in the yard. The first man had roped her, but Thowra did not know this. He called in answer, but she still did not come. He galloped towards the trees, hearing the men getting saddles and bridles. But a brumby stallion who knew the country would get a good start while they saddled up. He raced away towards the Cascades, taking the opposite direction to that in which his herd lay, the one the men might easily expect him to take.

Through the night he galloped, darkness like a curtain around him. A white owl flew, crying, from a tree and he shied in sudden fear. He could hear the men close behind, so he branched off the track and down a rock gully; the men, when they found they could not easily capture him, soon gave up. The owner of Golden had no wish to lame her in a midnight brumby hunt, and anyway it was obvious that Golden might very well bait a trap for Thowra. They decided to stay at the hut another night.

In the morning they built up the rails on the lowest side of the yard.

Thowra watched the track to Groggin and knew that they had not gone down from the mountain; he watched the sky, too, because he could see that bad weather was coming, and sensed that it was coming very quickly. When the men had not gone by mid-afternoon, he hastened off to his herd and took them lower down the Crackenback, where, if there were snow, they would be sheltered. Before they had reached the glade to which he was taking them, the wind was howling over the mountain-top and bringing with it biting flakes of snow. The foals were frightened and kept getting under their mothers' feet. Thowra felt responsible for them and stayed with them in the gathering storm. His knees were bruised and stiff from their rap on the fence, and he was glad to be with his mares.

All night long the cold snow fell. At Dead Horse Hut the men gave up hoping for the cream stallion to come, and worried about their own horses. The pack-horses were better off than the two riding-horses because there were trees in the paddock under which they could shelter.

Golden's owner was particularly worried. There was not room for even one horse to stand in the skillion; it was full of wood and bags of salt.

At midnight they decided to turn them out of the yard into the horse paddock. Already the snow lay inches deep on the ground; covered rails and fence-posts; slithered with a soft thud off the trees. The cream filly and the bay horse walked gladly through the gate and towards a clump of trees.

The men sloshed their way through the snow back to the hut, shook the flakes off their coats, threw more wood on the fire, and settled down again for what remained of the night.

It was in the heavy, dark hours of the very early morning, when the blizzard was at its height, that Thowra came.

He had to walk right to the yard before he was sure it was empty, then he went, silent-footed in the snow, right up to the skillion, but there was nothing there. He went back to the horse-paddock fence and followed it till it went through some trees. Here he could hear the snuffling and shuffling of quite a number of horses and guessed Golden would be with them.

He retreated a little way until he found a panel of fencing over which he thought he might be able to jump — it was not so much the height of the fence that bothered him, but rather where it was and where to jump — in the blizzard it was difficult to see anything clearly. He cantered towards it, making an enormous leap.

The snow beat in his eyes, hit his legs, his chest, his belly. He was flying through the blizzard — waiting for the ghastly check of biting barbed wire if he had miscalculated his jump. But there was no check, no terrible bite of wire on his legs. He slithered a little on landing and drew a huge breath of relief. He was safely over!

He jogged down the fence line until he came to the trees, then sneaked in, moving silently from tree to tree, conscious of every sound, feeling the cold touch of the snow on his coat. It was easy to see the dark-coloured horses, as he drew close to them, but Golden, like himself, was invisible in the snowstorm, and it was Golden he must find.

He had circled right round the group of horses before he found her, standing on her own under a tree by the fence. Straining his eyes, he could just see her outline, sensed that she had become suddenly tense, and he knew then that she had seen him. She stood quite still.

"Will you follow me, now?" he asked. "I will jump the fence and stand beside it so that you can see where it is. This fence is not too high for you to jump."

He could tell she was trembling with nervousness, but he did not understand that she was torn between her desire to go with him and her instinct to stay obediently where she was.

He moved off and she followed, back to the panel in the fence which he had jumped before. He took her to the fence and told her to make certain she knew how high she must leap.

The snow was driving behind Thowra this time; the wind almost lifted him, and he was so excited that he felt no fear of jumping too early or too late, or not high enough. When he landed he turned back and stood by the fence, neighing softly. For a moment he thought that Golden would not come; then she came, invisible – though he could hear her galloping – till she was right at the fence and taking off in a wildly high jump. She, too, was over and free. He led her off through the bush.

Cuscus

Chapter Sixteen

CHALLENGE AND ESCAPE

THROUGH THE SNOWSTORM Thowra led Golden. He was so wildly elated with his success in freeing her that he could hardly forbear from jumping up on a high rock to trumpet his joy in victory, and to set the echoes ringing in the hills. When he heard a dingo howl close by, he longed to roar back at him – and never realized that Golden was shaking with fear at the sound of the wild dog. He led her steadily back to the herd and got there as the first eerie, snow-filled light of the dawn came over the hills.

All the mares snuffled Golden curiously, while she stayed nervously by Thowra's side, but he would not let them waste time getting acquainted. As soon as the men missed Golden they would be after her. There was no time to lose; they must go as fast as the foals could travel, over to the Brindle Bull.

Challenge and Escape

It was necessary to cross the Crackenback much higher than usual because it was foaming full. Even then the first place he tried was too deep and swift for the foals, and they had to go higher still – and nearer to the men. Then Thowra found a crossing that he decided would have to do.

The snow was still falling, hitting the water and vanishing away. The anxious mares whinnied as he went across, the water foaming above his knees and nearly to his girth – white foam and grey, swirling water. He called to his mares. Golden had followed him closely, but those with foals stood and looked. Then the grey mare with her creamy foal started in, keeping the young one on the upstream side. She went very slowly, anxiously nuzzling at her foal and urging him on as his long legs slipped and stumbled among the slippery boulders. Then the force of the current hit them and the foal fell. He neighed with terror as he struggled to his feet. Thowra went in to try and help.

"Go back," Thowra commanded, for the first time feeling a compassionate interest in his sons and daughters, but realizing what a problem they could be if there were a real hunt for him and Golden. He could dimly remember – or remember from the tales Bel Bel had told him – the great brumby drive on Paddy Rush's Bogong when he himself was little bigger than his own foals.

Up the bank of the river they trekked, drawing ever closer to the men. At last, Thowra found a place that was possible, and escorted each mare and foal across, the little dun foals, all wet and bedraggled, looking more mousy than ever.

They had only just reached the safe covering of the bush when something made Thowra look higher up the stream, and there, through a thin curtain of falling snow, he could see a man, the one who usually rode Golden, sitting on the bay horse. Obviously he hadn't seen them or he would have been after them already, but he might see them if they started to move.

"Stand still!" he told his herd. "Don't move at all!" But it was all very well to say this; there were tired, fidgety foals to be considered. The dun-coloured ones would not show up, but restless little creamy would, and Golden, if she did not understand. But Golden was staying very quiet; she began to tremble violently as she recognized her master.

And again Thowra did not understand how torn she was between her loyalty to the man who had trained and fed her, and her longing to be with him, the wonderful silver stallion of whom all the horses, all the cattle, all the men spoke.

Just then the snow started to fall more heavily. Thowra drew his herd further into the bush while they were hidden by the snowstorm, but he could hear the man coming. He thought how, if he had been alone, he would have remained absolutely still and absolutely silent so that the man could have passed quite close and never seen him, but a herd of ten was not easily hidden. The only thing he could think of was to act as a decoy himself, lead the man off away from the herd.

He turned to Boon Boon, the creamy's dam, and told her to take the herd up to The Brolga's grazing ground, near the very top – knowing that The Brolga was still in the Cascades. Then he told Golden not to leave Boon Boon for a minute, and he went off silently, taking a direction that would bring him just ahead of the man, although he would still have the shelter of fairly thick timber. He wanted to be seen but not so well seen that the man would realize he had not got Golden with him.

He faded through the bush, listening, listening, and when he heard the horse quite close, he walked quietly through the trees so that he was just in front of the man.

There was a clatter of horse's shoes on rock as the man spurred his mount. Thowra bounded away. He knew he must keep his pursuer encouraged, and yet he must not let himself be caught; he must lead him right away from the herd.

It was madly exciting to see how near he could let that man come, and still allow time to dodge him. The rougher the country, the better he could dodge: the bay horse was not much good on steep, stony places.

To the man, Thowra must have been like a will-o'-the-wisp leading him on through the storm, sometimes just visible – a creamy flash, or two creamy flashes – sometimes there was just the sound ahead of branches swishing or of hooves on stones. The man could never have told, in that beating snow, if Golden were there or not. Once, Thowra deliberately neighed twice, as though he were calling Golden and she answering.

At last, he was approaching the place he had been making for – a long, long steep gully that went right down one side of the mountain and dropped off into sheer space. This gully was full of boulders and small stones. Thowra had only been down it once, with Storm, and had thought then that it might be a good place in which to escape from a man hunt. Very few tame horses carrying a heavy load could get down it without laming themselves, and, even if they did, there was no track leading off. He and Storm had found a way through huge rocks and dense heather to the foot of a waterfall, but it had taken a long time to find it, and there was nothing to mark the place.

There it was, the top of the gully; the storm was slackening slightly, and a faint tinge of blue was in the sky. He must hurry because the falling snow would help to hide him.

Down the snow-slippery rocks he went, slowly at first, to make sure the man was following, but keeping himself partly out of sight. Then, when the bay horse was quite close, he charged off, leaping and flying, almost trusting to the air more than the slippery leg-breaking rocks. He gave a mocking neigh. This was like leading Arrow on! Even if the man discovered now that Golden was not with him, he must be made to follow.

Down, down he went. Sometimes he felt a sickening jar when he did not land squarely on a rock, or when a rock rolled, but it was not for nothing that Bel Bel had taught him to flee like the wind through the roughest country.

Down, down, down, and the snow was still blowing in blinding flurries. He checked his speed because the man had dropped back. Now there was no sound of a horse clattering behind him, so he stopped and looked around.

The man was on the ground; he was looking at the bay's leg, at the hoof, feeling the tendons, feeling the knee, even running his hand over the shoulder.

"Looks like the end of him for a while," thought Thowra, and went steadily on downwards, until he found the way through the waterfall. He had a drink and crossed the stream, then went silently and tracklessly up and up the mountain towards the very top, to the camping grounds of The Brolga, where the herd should be grazing in safety.

The snow stopped, but an ice-cold wind blew the already fallen snow like sharp pebbles that stung against his coat and in his eyes. As much as possible he kept in the trees. It was nearly evening when he reached the grazing ground. There, in the grassy basin, he saw his grey mares and his foals, his black mare, and the lovely creamy filly he had stolen from the stockmen.

Of them all, perhaps Golden was gladdest to see him. It had been an anxious day for her, though Boon Boon had been friendly enough and had explained what Thowra was doing. But the others had ignored her, or sometimes given her a nip. Also she had found it hard work to follow them fast and keep quiet, as Boon Boon insisted she must, and leave no tracks. In fact, it was almost impossible for her to leave no hoofmarks because of her shining silver shoes, though one of these had already come off on the rough rocks.

Now, when she saw Thowra, she whinnied and trotted over to him.

Thowra nuzzled her, relieved and thankful to find her

there; he had been afraid that she would not follow the herd without him.

Thowra, of course, never bothered himself about how the man would get back to the hut, or how the two of them would leave the mountains, with one horse vanished and one lame, but he did think that it would be quite a long time before anyone molested them again.

For days of lovely sunny weather, with no snow on the lower mountains, they grazed on the Brindle Bull. The foals played and learnt to eat grass. Golden lost all but one front shoe, and tried to learn to be quieter and to keep herself hidden in the trees, but the ways of the wild country need a life-time of practice, and she had only been trained to carry a man on her back and do as he made her do.

Away from the Main Range, Thowra did not know what was going on, and did not see the first small mob of cattle come early to the Cascades. He was amazed, late one evening, not quite two weeks after he had captured Golden, to hear a tremendous stallion roar from the rim of the basin above him, and see, standing silhouetted against the blue-gold sky, The Brolga.

Thowra, like The Brolga, had once been with Yarraman, and was too full of his own strength and vigour to run away. He turned to Boon Boon telling her to start the herd for Paddy Rush's Bogong, then he went prancing and high-stepping forward to meet the great grey horse.

He did not notice that his own fine herd had only withdrawn to the rim of the basin, or that The Brolga's herd were lining the opposite rim, forming an audience for the big green amphitheatre in which he was going to fight. He kept prancing forward, and The Brolga came rearing and screaming towards him.

The green basin in the hills was filled with the last of the sunlight as the two horses, the enormous grey and the lithe, swift creamy, met. Sunlight glanced off them — spears of light shooting from Thowra's tossing mane — as the two wheeled and danced round each other without placing a blow.

It was natural that The Brolga should feel completely confident, just as it was natural that Thowra, in his first pride of being a stallion with a herd and foals of his own, should feel unbeatable, but those few moments of dancing and dodging The Brolga's forefeet calmed Thowra down enough for Bel Bel's teaching and her cunning to reassert itself. He realized that only his swiftness of movement was going to save him.

If The Brolga had not caught sight of Golden he might easily have got tired of trying to fight a nimble, flashing gadfly, but he had seen the beautiful creamy filly and wanted her for his herd.

He made a dash at Thowra, teeth bared; but Thowra was no longer in the same place. The Brolga pivoted on his great, powerful hind legs and struck rapidly with both forelegs. But Thowra had gone again and, in going, placed a resounding kick on the big grey rump.

This time Thowra retreated further and waited for The Brolga's advance. He had noted with annoyance how Boon Boon was letting the herd stand still and watch. Now he would have to lead The Brolga in another direction. This time, he did not dodge quick enough and received a stunning blow on the side of the head. He shook his head, jumped to one side and charged The Brolga himself, with a well-placed forefoot. Then away again.

The Brolga, unlike Arrow, did not waste his energy in rage, or in galloping after him. He followed slowly, rearing and snorting. Thowra knew he might never tire him, but he could lead him on to the rim of the basin, timing their arrival there for the fall of night. In darkness he should be able to escape and, he hoped, join his herd. Surely Boon Boon would understand what he was doing and get the herd away.

The Brolga saw what he was doing before Boon Boon did, and suddenly the big grey stallion left Thowra and started trotting to where the grey mares and the beautiful creamy were still outlined against the evening sky.

Boon Boon remembered how her father, The Brolga, had valued the creamy mare, Bel Bel, above all his herd. Immediately she saw him coming, she realized that he was after Golden, and she hustled the herd down into the timber and away.

The Brolga broke into a gallop, but Thowra was catching up, then racing past, placing a thundering kick on his shoulder and foreleg. For a while The Brolga took no notice of the madly galloping and kicking creamy stallion, but pursued the disappearing herd.

Thowra was desperate. It would be frightful to have captured Golden from the stockmen and then to lose her to this same stallion whom he had seen kill his own father. He knew he could gallop faster and dodge more nimbly than The Brolga, so after another really fierce kick at his chest, he raced past him and then turned to confront him.

The Brolga gave a cry of anger, rose on his hind legs, and struck. Once again Thowra was not there to be struck. The Brolga rushed forward again, after the herd, but Thowra was back in front of him. The grey came quietly and steadily onward, this time, the whites of his eyes showing, and his mouth open. Thowra danced away. The light was fading, and he would be able to escape to his herd if only he could keep "playing" The Brolga for a little longer. He danced, he dodged, he kicked, while the big grey stallion kept forcing his way in the direction in which the herd had gone, but all the time it grew darker.

Thowra's eyes were too good for The Brolga to gain much advantage from his colour fading into the on-coming dark, but sometimes, when the big horse moved swiftly and came from an unexpected angle, he was like a ghost, without substance in the night. Then, just for a few minutes, The Brolga did have all the advantage. It was almost completely dark, but Thowra's light colour still showed more clearly, and The Brolga came at him to give him a real beating. Thowra received some tremendous blows but always he just managed to avoid The Brolga's bite. When he reckoned his herd must be well away then he started to dance off in another direction.

The Brolga suddenly gave up the idea of catching Golden that night, and when a ringing neigh echoed round and round the basin, he stopped chasing Thowra to listen. It came again from the direction of his own herd. Thowra heard it and knew that it was Bel Bel, his mother, calling The Brolga away. The galloping hooves behind him stopped, but Thowra kept on until he reached the rim of the basin. There he threw up his head and neighed once to Bel Bel before galloping down, swinging round, when he was sure he was not being followed, in the direction his herd would have taken for Paddy Rush's Bogong.

Black Cockatoo

Chapter Seventeen

THOWRA IN FLIGHT

NOW THAT ARROW was dead, Thowra could be undisputed king of any other stallions who spent the summer with his herd on Paddy Rush's Bogong, and there was more room there than on the Brindle Bull. Pleased to be going there, he led his mares to the old grazing ground where he had been with Yarraman's herd when he was as small as his own foals.

It was exciting, too, going over all the country that he and Storm had explored; finding some scrub grown far thicker, some burnt and offering no cover at all; finding again the rock paths and the ravine where they had lost Arrow.

He examined very closely the cliff that Bel Bel and Mirri had once made them jump down to avoid the manhunt, and realized it still offered a good place of escape.

He showed it to Golden and taught her how to make the twisting jump that was needed, then showed her the way into the scrub. Always he was teaching her to be quiet and try and leave no track, and at last she had lost the fourth shoe.

Boon Boon, with her cream foal, might become the object of a hunt, too, so she also tried to jump down the cliff, and then took her foal over it.

Every day, Thowra went to a vantage spot where he could look out over the Crackenback towards the Dead Horse Hut, and spent hours watching. Somehow he was sure the owner of Golden would not be long in returning. And only about five days after they had reached Paddy Rush's Bogong, he saw the far-away specks of men on horseback heading towards the Brindle Bull. Just for a moment they were visible, then they had vanished into the bush. He went back to the herd and took them off into some almost impenetrable scrub, the snowgums and heather closing around them and leaving no trace.

There was a tiny clearing on the banks of a creek, inside their hiding-place; and the foals lay there, beside their mothers, while the mares and stallion listened and listened all day long.

At night they all crept out to feed with the shy wombats and wallabies, and listened to the mopokes calling. Just before dawn, they were hidden again in the silent, aromatic scrub. Another day started to pass very slowly. The sky had become grey-milky, and the black cockatoos were crying in the trees. The still air in their clearing became very oppressive. Thowra felt his coat pricking uncomfortably. It was too still, and the cockatoos' cry was full of foreboding. He wished he knew what was happening on the Brindle Bull.

The wind started to blow, hot and menacing, and the silence was broken by the roar it made through the trees, by the groaning, lashing boughs. Thowra was now thoroughly uncomfortable. Even through the torrent of sound made by the storm he thought he could hear movement on the mountain – not galloping, but animals creeping, hiding.

Ordering the herd to stay absolutely quiet, he went cautiously out through the dense scrub, working this way and that so that he could be sure no enemies were approaching through the cover to their hiding place. He saw nothing until he reached the very edge of the belt of timber and heather. The long, clear glade beyond was empty, but, moving along through the next belt of trees, he could see, in amongst the bending, wind–contorted limbs, a file of horses, with small grey foals beside their mothers, and there, in the lead, just behind The Brolga, was his own mother, Bel Bel.

Something must have made Bel Bel look in his direction. He was sure he was hidden from sight, but it was as though she looked through all the leaves and heather hiding him, and saw his eyes. She moved her head in a nod of recognition, but made no other sign.

Thowra went back to his herd. That night he would not let them go out to graze. Tremendous rain started soon after dark, and they took shelter under the thick trees, but they were all getting hungry and restless. Thowra himself wandered to and fro through the scrub.

At last, after midnight, he saw Bel Bel coming through the rain and the darkness, through the grotesquely moving trees.

"Well, my son of the wind and the rain and the storm," she said, "it would seem as if you have brought more than a little trouble on us all through stealing this filly from the men."

"What has happened?" asked Thowra.

"The Brolga is very angry," she said. "The men came, creeping, searching, trying to find you and this filly they call Golden. There were men everywhere. At first they did not bother about us, but then perhaps they were angry that they did not find you, and they started chasing and roping. That's why we left. Next they will come here. You will have to go farther away."

"I know this mountain and all its hiding-places very well," Thowra said.

"Yes, my son, I know you do, but there are a lot of you to hide. You will have to go farther down the river. The country is rough there and the grazing is not good, but it would be better to have a summer of poor food – and to remain free."

As she spoke Thowra saw the fire and sparkle in her eyes. She was old now, but the courage of the "lone wolf" mare was undiminished.

"Where is Mirri?" he asked suddenly.

"Mirri died last year," Bel Bel answered sadly. "It will be my turn soon, but I have a great wish that my bones should bleach up high on the Ramshead."

"And mine, too, some day," Thowra said. "What does The Brolga mean to do now? Stay here, or go back to his grounds on the Brindle Bull?"

"I don't know. He may fancy this mountain and hunt you out."

"Hunt me out!"

"Yes. You couldn't beat him in a fight. He'd like Golden, too, you know that."

"Oh well," Thowra said. "I'll wait and see where he goes, and what the men do."

"I wouldn't wait. I'd go before the men come after you because of your beautiful cream hide and the filly's, or before The Brolga kills you for both." And Bel Bel was gone as silently as she had come, fading into the dark and the storm, vanishing behind the beating, wind-twisted boughs of the snowgums.

Thowra thought over what she had said. His mother knew so much, and all she had taught him had been good. He knew it would be better to go now, taking his herd away under cover of the night and the wild rain.

Ghost-like, he flitted back through the scrub: like ghosts his herd followed him out, and followed him all through the night, up and down steep slopes, over rocks, across streams, along the soft snowgrass glades, around the top of Paddy Rush's Bogong and down the other side: up and down and along ever rougher and rougher country.

Dawn came, and across a break in the stormy eastern sky a flight of brown teal winged their way. There was water close, plenty of water, in the Crackenback River and many small creeks, but the grass grew only in odd tussocks, and the herd was very hungry.

Thowra led them on and on. Somewhere, he thought, there must be better grazing than this. Down on the river there might be more grass, but men came there. The only thing to do was to cut away from the river, and see what lay in the hills.

In the weeks that followed, Thowra taught Golden all he could about the bush, about keeping herself hidden, about making no sound, and leaving no track.

One night, Boon Boon came to him.

"There is not enough food here for mares that are feeding hungry foals," she said. "We are getting thin and weak, and our foals do not grow enough."

Thowra, too, was tired of the rough, uninteresting country, and of always feeling hungry.

"We will go then," he said, "back to Paddy Rush's Bogong."

When they got back to the mountains, he did not lead his herd straight to the grazing grounds. He left them hidden some distance away, and went up himself, late in the evening, examining the ground, the grass, the shrubs, all the way for any tracks of other horses, wild or tame. The only signs he saw were weeks old. When he carefully peered into the grazing ground, there was no one there, and as he walked all over it, looking and sniffing with the greatest thoroughness, he realized that no horses had been there for at least three weeks.

He went back for the herd.

After the sparse grazing on the hills down the river, the mares never lifted their heads from the sweet grass. They fed all day without ceasing. Thowra and Golden, too, were very hungry, but not with the urgent hunger of the mares with foals at foot, so when Thowra started off to have another look round, Golden followed him.

Only scattered cattle could be seen over on the Main Range, but down on the crossing of the Crackenback there was a small mob of horses.

"Storm!" said Thowra excitedly, and started down to meet him, as usual going where he could leave no tracks and in timber where he would be invisible from the other side of the river.

It was late afternoon when the two horses met. Red sunlight gilded Thowra as he advanced, playfully rearing, to meet his half-brother, his brother of the wind and the rain.

Storm reared up, too, a magnificent bay horse now, and they nipped each other joyfully, cavorted and danced. At last, when their greetings were over, Thowra asked:

"Are you coming to the grazing ground?"

"For a night or perhaps two," Storm answered. "The men seek everywhere for you and Golden, and anyway there will be too many of us."

As they climbed up the hill, Thowra reflected how his theft of Golden had made life very dangerous and uncomfortable – how everyone said so, and yet no one seemed to blame him for taking her. He remembered that night at the Dead Horse hut, when he had first rubbed noses with her through the rails, and knew he would steal her all over again if he had to. He looked back at her, saw her putting her neat hooves carefully where he put his, saw her outlined in burning gold by the setting sun. She was lovely, and she was his.

Storm had four mares and foals with him. It would mean quite a number of them on the grazing ground if they all stayed together. Storm was probably wise not to stay long, but now that they were together, he realized how much he had missed his company.

"Where have you just come from?" he asked Storm.

"The back of the Brindle Bull."

"What's going on there?"

"Well, men are always appearing everywhere. They don't bother about us ordinary-coloured horses, but they make things pretty uncertain. Also, there's no room for anyone else but The Brolga there." Then, as he walked along beside Thowra, he added: "I didn't really expect to find you here. Wouldn't be surprised if The Brolga doesn't come over and fight you for Golden — and, anyway, the men will come here soon."

"Couldn't find enough good grass anywhere else, but I like this country," said Thowra, "and I know all the hiding places."

They went steadily on up the hill, not hurrying the mares and foals, and keeping well inside the timber. They did not see a man sitting absolutely still on a chestnut horse high up on a rocky crag. The man stared and stared at the movement in the timber, then he, too, went on up the mountain.

Only a man who had begun to know something of the silver brumby's cunning would have guessed that he was there in the trees – that the faint suggestion of movement in the timber meant horses led by "Silver". This man was Thowra's old enemy, the man on the black horse. The last of the daylight went, then, but the man had seen enough.

About an hour later, an almost full moon rose over the eastern hills, throwing its eerie light into the clearings and long glades, making strange shadows among the trees, leaving pools of darkness in deep hollows or gullies. The wild horses went on up through the timber, never having to move in clear country until they were nearly at the grazing ground.

As a matter of course, Thowra stopped and looked cautiously out through the trees before he led the other horses into the bright moonlight. This time the man was well hidden, and he saw clearly the beautiful cream stallion step out of the trees; and the man held his breath when he saw, just behind the stallion, the filly, Golden.

The horses went through the moonlit clearing and into a gully filled with black sallee trees and were lost to view again, among the long, drooping leaves, the dark boughs and trunks, the festoons of old man's beard.

The man waited a while and then rode across the clear ground into the black sallees and followed the horses up the hill.

The herd was peacefully spread out in the wide valley when Thowra got back to them. Little foals lay asleep on the grass, sleeping mares standing over them. But Boon Boon was wide awake and neighing softly. When she saw the number of horses with Thowra she moved nervously around and stood over her little creamy foal. When they were all down in the moon-filled valley there was quite a mob of horses.

It was Thowra who heard the jangle of a bit first. He looked up, saw the horse and its rider.

"Go!" he urged. "Go all ways! Don't stay together!" When Golden tried to come with him he bared his teeth and turned her in another direction. A man by himself might get confused in the moonlight, and be unable to make up his mind which horse to follow. If he chased Golden, Thowra thought he might manage to cut in and confuse him – and he felt extremely confident of evading a rope.

The man did chase Golden, of course. He had made up his mind to go for her, thinking that perhaps if he caught her and tied her up, he might get her brumby stallion later. He was gaining on Golden, and had got his lasso ready, when there were suddenly two creamies galloping ahead of him, and, as soon as the second one was there, they began to twist and weave, and dodge in a way that made it almost impossible to keep them separate in his mind. But this man had learnt a lot since he first used to hunt Thowra. For one thing, he had become skilled with the rope. Several times, as they galloped, he could have lassoed Thowra – and Thowra knew this – but it was Golden he really wanted.

Just before they reached the trees would be the danger time. Then, Thowra knew, the man might rope either of them rather than lose both.

Thowra's heart was thudding with fear and anger. The line of trees, black in the moonlight, was still some yards off. The man was almost alongside.

"Prop and swing right round, then towards the trees again," he told Golden, and propped, swinging himself straight across the front of the pursuing horse.

The man must have thought very quickly and decided that he would not now get Golden before she reached the timber and its concealing shadows. The rope went whistling through the moonlight and round Thowra's neck.

With a squeal of rage and terror the stallion galloped faster than he had ever galloped before, straight for the trees, and instead of being able to hold him, the man and his horse had to go off with him in his crazy gallop.

Thowra, maddened by the cutting rope on his neck, and the sudden, desperate fear of being caught, could only think of the trees, and the sheltering darkness underneath them. With branches stinging his face, his flanks, and whipping down his rump, he raced in among them. He was too frightened to plan, but without thinking lowered his head, and shot down a tunnel in the snowgums.

He could hear a great crashing behind him and the man's voice. Then the rope went slack. For a while he barely understood that the man was no longer holding him. The rope was still round his neck, terrifying him.

Often the end of it caught on something, and pulled him up with a jerk. He did not realize his danger, but kept on in his wild flight. At last he calmed down; there was no longer a horse following him; slowly he slackened speed and stopped. By a miracle the trailing end of rope was still hanging free. Now he tried to get it off, but the noose had pulled tight around his neck and he couldn't loosen it. He tried desperately to shake it off, not wanting to waste time in case the man followed him again. Also, he wondered where Golden was.

He struck across the hillside through the timber, but by now he was able to understand from the snagging of the long rope that, for once, he would be safer in the open grass country. Out in the long glade he trotted in a direction he hoped might lead him to Golden. He knew she would stay in the timber and wondered whether it was safe to neigh softly sometimes – otherwise he might miss her.

He neighed and stood still to listen. There was no sound, no sound to the side or in front of him, and no sound from behind where the man must be.

Trees threw long shadows across the glade. Within the timber there was heavy darkness, but on the outer fringe each tree danced, silver in a soft breeze, like living things, the moving legs of a hundred creamy horses dancing to mountain music.

Thowra trotted on. Before he had gone very far he stopped and neighed again, his ears trembling forward to catch the faintest reply. Then, ah, then, it came on the breeze, and it was definitely Golden answering, and presently he heard the deeper call of Boon Boon.

With a snort of relief, Thowra broke into a canter, though not so fast that he would be brought up with a terrible jerk if the rope caught in a bush.

He neighed again, once, and they answered him: then at last he was with them. Boon Boon propped and shied away as she saw the rope trailing from his neck, but Golden nibbled at his shoulder for a second and then set to purposefully with her teeth to undo the tight slip knot.

He was free! The scent on the breeze was sweeter, the cold glitter of moonlight on the free-fluttering leaves was thrilling, the touch of the snowgrass underfoot, and the sweet taste of the creekwater – all perhaps better than they had ever been before.

Thowra drank and drank, as though he would fill his whole self with the freedom he had so nearly lost.

Lyrebird

Chapter Eighteen

HORSE HUNT: MAN HUNT

THAT NIGHT THOWRA'S herd did not gather all together, and in the morning he went back to the grazing ground to see if he could find them.

The air was fresh and clear, renewed by the night. Thowra felt his old urge to leap on to the top of a crag and trumpet out his joy in being alive and free. He saw little curls of mist rise up from the river and puff away into nothingness in the breeze; he heard lyrebirds calling in the thickets round a creek, and his heart seemed to stop for a second when one mimicked the crack of a stickwhip. Then he lost his panic as the mimicking voice whistled and then barked like a dog. The man had never had a dog; it was just Menura, the lyrebird, having fun in the bright early morning.

He moved so quietly and carefully that a dingo bitch

playing with her fat puppies in a patch of sunlight did not hear him coming.

"Never mind, old woman, I won't hurt your beautiful children," he said to her. "Tell me, have you seen sign of man near here?"

"A man on his own two legs went towards the river a mile from here, leading a lame horse, late last night. You will smell his blood, maybe. He had cut his head, and his horse, too, bled from the shoulder."

Thowra nodded his thanks, snuffed at the pups, and said again, with much politeness, how beautiful they were. Then he went on his way with more confidence.

He came on the man's trail, and shied with sudden fear at the smell. A jay mocked him from the trees above.

There was still no sign of the three missing mares and their foals, or of Storm and his herd.

A silent gang-gang threw a gum-nut down on to his back. Thowra jumped and then shook himself with annoyance. Up above him, from the direction of the grazing ground, he suddenly heard a sound that made his coat prickle and the sweat break out behind his ears. He went on with far greater caution than before, circling round a little so that he could look into the grazing ground from the dense cover of some scrub.

The green valley lay below him, filled with early morning sunshine – and with a mob of horses. Running excitedly to and fro, sniffing at every trail, was The Brolga.

Thowra stood absolutely still. He knew he was hidden by snowgum branches, that he must have time to see if his own mares were there, and think what to do next. He peered through the thick leaves and soon saw that his own mares were not there. He also saw that Bel Bel was not with The Brolga's herd and wondered if she had gone to warn him, or simply remained at the Brindle Bull.

Then he saw The Brolga pick up the trail he had made with Golden the night before, and the trail of the man chasing them. Now he knew he would have to move, and very quickly, or The Brolga might find what remained of his herd. He hurried away, as fast as he could go without making a noise or leaving a trace.

He went in as straight a line as he could towards the place where he had left Golden and Boon Boon, and all the time he listened, he looked, and he sniffed the keen air for any strange scent that would tell him The Brolga – or anyone else – was near. Twice, a long way ahead of him, he thought he saw something moving, but he decided it might be a silver-grey kangaroo, or perhaps just a shadow. Then he saw it again. He looked at the ground: there was no track. He stopped and listened: there was no sound. He sniffed and just then the breeze blew back to him. Unmistakably came the scent, a scent he knew well, a scent that rose right out of his eternal memory. His nostrils quivered, his top lip curled right back. Who was it? And then, of course, he knew. Bel Bel was ahead of him. He went on, faster, to catch her.

He saw her, fairly clearly ahead, saw her suddenly swing round and listen. He showed himself, and they trotted to meet each other.

"Where are you going, little old mother?" he asked.

"Searching for you, my son, to bring you warning."

"I have seen The Brolga," said Thowra, "and he is already on to the trail that Golden and I left last night when a man chased us. I go to join what is left of my herd, and I must waste no time."

"I will come with you a little way."

They trotted on together through the trees and through the mint bush that was starred with pink-mauve flowers. Here the trees' bark was splashed with red and green. There it was pure silver where a clear creek crossed their path, and where there was a spongy swamp over which they must not leave a track.

"Soon I must turn back," said Bel Bel, "but, before I leave you, tell me, where are you going to take your herd?"

"Over to the hanging valley on the Brindle Bull, and when The Brolga goes away from here, we shall return."

"This year you must not fight him again," Bel Bel answered. "Next year you will have reached your full strength."

"I am faster than he," said Thowra.

"Next time you fight him," Bel Bel said, "it will be either you or The Brolga, so before you fight again be sure you have all your strength and all your cunning. I must go now." She nuzzled him briefly on the wither, and then went off through the trees.

Thowra looked back over his shoulder several times and saw her still trotting on and then vanishing from sight. It did not seem strange to him that he and his mother had never forgotten each other. Other mares forgot their foals, foals forgot their mothers, but Bel Bel, the creamy mare, had never forgotten her cream colt foal, nor had he forgotten her, though he was now a stallion almost at his full strength.

He hurried on. The Brolga, with no need to hide his tracks, might go faster than he – and The Brolga must not find Golden and Boon Boon. Bel Bel was right; if he and The Brolga fought now for Golden, The Brolga would surely kill him. Thowra did reach Golden and Boon Boon before The Brolga found them, but up the hillside he could hear the big grey stallion, still following the trail.

Thankfully, he saw that the rest of his herd were with the two mares. Without wasting a moment, he mustered them and drew them back up the hill and round on to the Crackenback Fall. He had to risk their movement through the bush being seen by any men over on the Main Range, rather than risk passing too close to The Brolga and having him pick up their tracks immediately.

It was just bad luck that one of the foals started a rock rolling down a long, stony slope, and worse luck that the rock kept going and gaining speed and collecting other leaping, skipping stones with it so that there was quite a clatter. There was more than enough noise to make The Brolga stop and listen. Just then a gust of wind had to blow sharply from the north-west and carry their scent straight to the trembling, sniffing grey nostrils.

Thowra heard the snort of breath being drawn through those back-curled nostrils, and knew The Brolga would be after them. He looked around for the best line of country, and saw a long rocky spine, tree-covered and precipitous — a place where the nimblest-footed horse would have a big advantage. A windhover was gliding over it.

"The Ridge of the Hawk," thought Thowra. "That is the place for me." He turned to the mares: "Now go," he said. "Go quietly but fast. Go to the hanging valley on the Brindle Bull and wait there for me. I may be a long time. I will stay here and try to get The Brolga to follow me, or I will fight and run, and fight and run, trying to stop him catching you. Go!"

He watched the mares and foals fade away through the bush, watched the creamy filly, Golden, as the sunlight dappled her in glory. Then they had gone, and he waited till he heard the sound of The Brolga coming. When he knew he was close, he went very quietly and hid in thick trees on the first knoll of the Ridge of the Hawk.

The Brolga cantered into view, fierce grey head up, ears pricked — listening, not watching the tracks.

To stop him looking down and possibly seeing where the herd had gone, Thowra kicked a rock and sent it bounding down the ridge.

The Brolga swung towards the sound. Thowra moved just enough for his creamy hide to show through the trees — to show twice — then he stood still.

The Brolga gathered himself into a grey curve, like an iron hoop, and shot towards the rocky ridge.

Thowra watched him, deep-chested, powerful, the great, strong legs stretching over snowgrass and bushes. Then he went tearing down the ridge, making enough noise for ten, not just for two.

He could hear The Brolga crashing down behind him, the heavier, older horse not managing to take the rough, steep ridge so fast. Just then, he saw that the ridge split into two a little distance below, and he determined to wait, where it divided, and see if The Brolga would go headlong past him.

He hid in a cleft between two immense rocks, having first kicked a collection of boulders down the northern-most ridge. The boulders bounded down as though a small herd of brumbies were flying down the ridge. The Brolga came, and then hurtled past. Thowra was just going to move out of his cleft in the rocks and go down the other ridge, when all of a sudden he heard The Brolga's headlong gallop slacken and stop, and, before he could get more than a few yards away from the division in the ridge, The Brolga, in a fury, was charging upwards again.

For a second, Thowra heard the echo of Bel Bel's voice in his ears – "*it will be either you or The Brolga*" – but he could not run away, for then The Brolga would soon guess that Golden was not with him, and start looking around for her tracks again. He would have to dodge and hide, take up as much time as he could, while the others got away, and lead The Brolga as far as possible from any tracks they might have left.

Quiet as a ghost, he moved among the rocks, always being careful to leave a way of escape behind as well as in front. Then he stood, trembling with excitement, his

beautiful silver-cream hide streaked darkly with sweat. The
Brolga was near the top. There was quiet for a minute,
perhaps for two minutes, and Thowra did not dare move
over to see where The Brolga was.

Something that was half a sound, or a sound he half
heard, seemed to be very near him. Then all of a sudden he
was staring into The Brolga's fierce eyes from behind the
rock. He just had time to notice the red, fiery flesh inside
the dilated grey nostrils before he had sprung backwards
into thick heather scrub, swung round and away. Only his
speed could save him now.

The Brolga was right behind him. Thowra felt his
breath, hot, scorching like a north wind, but he also felt his
own strength surge through him.

To the windhover that had returned and was hanging in
the air above the ridge it might have seemed a flashing
second in which either horse could have won the desperate
race – either the enormous, powerful grey, or the silver-
cream, so lithe and swift. That second, though, which
flashed past the hawk, was one of wild effort to the two
horses. The Brolga was straining every ounce of his great
strength to get close enough to Thowra to bite or strike:
Thowra was calling up reserves of energy that he had never
used before, trying, trying to leap away down the rocky
slope – to leap away and live. To each horse perhaps that
second seemed an hour, or a day, or a lifetime.

Suddenly Thowra felt himself as one steel ball, his legs
beneath him filled with an immeasurable power. He sprang,
cleaving the air, almost from underneath the bounding grey,

gathered himself together as he landed on a rock and sprang again. He was out of reach. A snowgum branch whipped him across the flanks, he smelt the tang of the leaves. Just behind he could hear The Brolga's breath, but each leap took him farther out of reach.

It was no use getting too far ahead, he knew. Soon would come the moment to stop and offer fight, to keep drawing The Brolga farther and farther away from the herd's tracks, lower and lower down the steep slope so that it would take him hours to climb back.

The Brolga was too angry to stop and think that it was really Golden he was after – or perhaps he felt in all his pounding blood that it was better to kill Thowra *now*. The screams of jays in a snowgum only made him angrier. He went plunging down, after Thowra, crashing and stumbling over the boulders.

Thowra, nimble and swift, kept ahead, just ahead.

Right down to the Crackenback they went, Thowra in the heat of the chase forgetting all about his first and oldest enemy – Man. And there, on the opposite bank, listening and watching, alert and on fairly fresh horses, were two men.

Thowra had seen the shining water and felt his body long to be in it. He had seen white sand stretching to the water at the crossing, and heather and the big white-flowered pimelia bush dipping to the water from the banks, but as he saw them he saw the men, and everything was instantly blurred by the horror of the situation. All he knew was that it would be better to go down-stream for a while, rather than try to get back uphill where the fresh horses would undoubtedly catch them very quickly. This all happened in one second – he saw the river, he saw the men, he forgot The Brolga, and he turned and fled.

The Brolga saw the men, and he turned, too, and followed Thowra as fast as he could go.

Clouds of white spray splashed up in the sunlight, as the men forced their horses fast through the river. Then there was a most fantastic chase that became a legend among men, with many of the other tales of Thowra's doings.

Thowra knew the country along the river well, and knew, too, many of the little valleys that stretched back into the hills where he and his herd had tried to find grass early in the spring. He thought he would keep to these valleys where tree ferns and logs had fallen, where tea-tree grew, covered with hanging moss and creepers, and the creeks wound invisible through this tangle of dead and living bush. He felt certain that he, so sure-footed and without a heavy man on his back, should be able to race even the far fresher horses through that leg-breaking, neck-breaking country.

When he was hard-pressed by The Brolga he had not thought about the men, and now, hard-pressed by men, he forgot about The Brolga. He went at truly breakneck speed along the banks of the Crackenback, waiting till he found the particular creek and fern-filled valley up which he intended to turn.

He clattered perilously around a rocky outcrop that overhung the foaming water, he forced a way through and over a mass of fallen trees and driftwood left by floods, and all the time he could hear the crashing and clattering behind him of the chase. Not much farther, and he could turn away from the river and into the dark cleft of the valley where the Christmas bush and tea-tree were flowering and where there was the hot, steamy smell of rotting fern, and wood, and leaves in the unmoving air.

His heart was thundering. How long it was that he had been galloping he did not know: he was tired, tired, tired, but at least Golden should be safely away by now, and Boon Boon and the other mares and foals.

The men were very close as he turned into the valley. He heard a rope whistle, and leapt into a great thicket of tree ferns.

In all the layers of rotten logs and the old fern trunks that were interlaced, to and fro, over the creek and across the valley floor, even Thowra stumbled and crashed, but he knew the men, with their tame horses, would never get through it as fast as he. There was hope now. He looked back once, just before he plunged into a tangle of the dark-barked swamp gum that was hung with green vines, laced with blanket-wood and bracken, and he saw the men, on two bay horses, saw the vivid colour of their check shirts – and then he saw The Brolga. What, oh what, was going to be the finish of this? If he got away from the men, could he ever get away from The Brolga? Would he escape only to be killed?

It was impossible to go very fast. Often he had to leap from one log to another; often he broke through rotting timbers into water or squelching black soil and steaming

leaf mould. The heat was oppressive in this valley where no
wind stirred, and Thowra had been forced to gallop twice
for his life; first last night, when he had, too, the terror of
being roped, and now, almost all the day, and he could feel
his strength ebbing. Always there was the sound behind of
the men and The Brolga.

The sweat streamed off him. He knew he must drink
soon. He made an enormous effort to get ahead enough to
have time to stop and drink. He looked back and could see
only one man behind The Brolga and both he and The
Brolga were sufficiently far behind to give him a moment
at a deep, dark pool. As he drank he wondered where the
other man was. If he had tried going higher up, in the hope
that the country would be so much clearer that he could
race ahead and get right around the two brumbies, Thowra
knew he was going to be disappointed; the sides of the
valley were all deeply cut by tiny gorges and creeks, each
one filled with a tangle of fallen timber or with rock rubble
and creepers.

Thowra drank with gasping gulps and then went on and
on, and anyone watching him – seeing the lovely cream
stallion leap on to a log, change feet and leap again, dance
through a trap of branches lying this way and that – would
hardly have known how exhausted he was. But, though he
gained on his pursuers, they still kept on coming. The chase
was like a fantastic nightmare, slow-moving because none of
the horses could go fast through the immense tangle.

At last he realized that there was much less noise behind
him. He looked around, standing for a moment with heaving

flanks, nostrils dilating with every shattering breath. There was only The Brolga to be seen, The Brolga following, following.

Half a mile further on, Thowra knew another valley that came in from the south. If he followed that it would give him a good short cut on the way back towards Golden and his herd on the Brindle Bull – but he was not going to let The Brolga follow him for ever. Exhaustion rose in waves through him, and anger at The Brolga for having kept up the chase for so long a time.

He came to a small, peaty clearing: there he stopped and waited, his head thrown up proudly, even though he gasped for breath – at least snatching a few minutes' rest while The Brolga plunged on up the valley through all the entanglement on the ground. As he stood waiting, the last glittering gleam reflected from the sunset died out of the valley.

Then a strange green glow began to flow through the deep valley; only the tall, slender ribbon gums stood out of the greenness in white majesty. Thowra looked around him, aware of the strange light, not knowing that he, too, stood out in pale splendour like the ribbon gums – the silver stallion indeed, as the men who had first seen him at night, by the light of the campfire, had named him.

There he stood, in the little clear patch of ground by the creek, surrounded by the interwoven green bush, with the tall white pillars of trees, and the green light. There he stood, waiting for The Brolga.

The Brolga came, striving to gallop towards his enemy, but slowed down by all the tangle on the valley floor. His breath was rasping in and out, and Thowra had had time for his own breathing to have lessened to deep, pounding breaths. He was exhausted and so was Thowra, but here, below the white ribbon gum pillars, with the flowing green light becoming deeper and deeper as evening approached, they must fight.

It was not the fight Bel Bel had prophesied – that was still to come: it was a weird fight between two horses that were too tired to hurt each other, a fight that went on, in silence, till they both dropped down at the farthest corners of the clearing, unable to move. Night came then, and the green light became grey, and then darkness covered the two stallions where they lay.

A fox barked nervously, and suddenly, from above, there was the chattering bark of a great, black flying phallanger silhouetted high up on the white trunk of a ribbon gum. The phallanger took off and went gliding right across the exhausted stallions. A mopoke, disturbed by his noise, gave his first call of the night: "Mopoke, Mopoke" echoing in the dark-enclosed valley.

Gradually, there came all the creeping, rustling sounds that are heard in the stillness of the night, as wombats climbed out of their holes and padded softly along a tree-trunk that formed a bridge across the creek, as possums climbed among leafy branches, as the snakes – the evil ones – wriggled along the leafy ground.

Thowra lay so still that a possum passed quite close as it went from tree to tree. Presently the exhaustion of the horses changed into deep sleep and they lay there, their feet still gathered underneath them, as they had dropped.

The slow hours of the night passed, the stars moved across the sky above the net of leaf and branch that was the ceiling of the valley, and even in such profound sleep Bel Bel's training, the birthright of cunning she had given Thowra, did not leave him. Before too many stars had slipped through the net above him, Thowra woke and got stiffly to his feet.

He looked over towards the heap in the darkness which was The Brolga, then moved silently away, turning up the southward valley that would take him on the first part of his journey towards the Brindle Bull and his herd. Like a pale, floating will-o'-the-wisp he went on and on through the night.

In the first grey dawn The Brolga woke and found himself alone, with no track to show him whither Thowra had gone; alone, and far, far from his own country.

Chapter Nineteen

NOW GOLDEN WAS THE PRIZE

SLOWLY, THROUGH THE bright, hot summer, yet another legend began to grow up round Thowra, a legend the men started to feel was true – and one that the horses believed absolutely.

Bad luck, it was said, came to everyone, either man or horse, who chased the silver brumby stallion. Had not men been hurt and their horses lamed? Had they not lost the beautiful filly, Golden? And Arrow, the horses said, Arrow had been killed. Surely this Thowra had a magic quality. Not only had he, when exhausted, got right away from two men on fresh horses, but he had vanished, simply vanished.

And just like the wind in a blizzard can twist and turn even wild horses until they are almost lost in the swirling snow, Thowra had twisted and turned The Brolga as they galloped, and The Brolga had woken in the weird first dawning, quite uncertain where he was.

Every horse was sure that Thowra, though a horse, was, in some magic way, the wind for which his mother had named him.

The men felt that something would surely happen to them if they chased him, but they could not resist the longing to try to catch him. The Brolga felt that Thowra would defeat him, in some very unusual manner, but he longed for revenge — and he longed to make Golden the pride of his herd.

All summer the stockmen and The Brolga sought for Thowra and, if they saw him, they chased him. All summer Thowra and his mares and foals were chased, but they always vanished. Sometimes they were heard, and yet not seen. If they left some tracks, these tracks would abruptly cease, as though they had all melted into the air. It was the mysteriousness of Thowra that made each stockman feel as if he must catch him.

Of all the horses running in the mountains, Bel Bel alone thought she knew the secret hiding-place that enabled Thowra and his herd to disappear from all their hunters. When she heard how Thowra and his mares vanished, she wondered if he had found again the deep valley that was like a cleft in the hills at the back of Paddy Rush's Bogong, the valley with the grassy Hidden Flat that could not be seen from the top. The valley where Yarraman and his herd had hidden after the men's brumby drive so many summers ago when Thowra and Storm were foals.

Old as she was, she decided to go off and see for herself if this was where he was hiding.

As she jogged along, purposefully through the bush, she came on fresh tracks and recognized the spoor as Storm's, so she followed him and found him with his mares, grazing peacefully. She whinnied and he lifted his noble bay head with a swift movement that reminded her of Mirri. In a moment, the big stallion was rubbing his nose on her neck.

"I go in search of Thowra," Bel Bel said.

"I, too, came this way feeling that I might find him," said Storm, "and yet I don't know why."

"If you come with me, I think you will remember why you have come this way." Bel Bel nodded her old head. "You have been here before, but you were very young, Mirri and I brought you here as two foals."

Thus it was that Storm set off with the old creamy mare, carefully following her trackless way, because he knew they must not lead either The Brolga or any wandering stockmen to Thowra's hiding-place.

Bel Bel scrambled down the cliff into the valley rather lower downstream than the grass flat, and she and Storm walked together up the rocky creekbed, or along narrow banks above the green water.

As she walked, Bel Bel was thinking that when autumn came she must go to the Ramshead Range, and there perhaps she would stay, for the time had come for the wild snow to cover her body. It was impossible that she should live as long as her cream and silver son. Perhaps, if she found him now, this would be the last time she would see him;

perhaps they would meet again, high on the Range, before the snows came.

When they rounded a bend in the rocky, foaming river, just where there were great high cliffs, they came on the Hidden Flat, a long, quite wide, green valley. Above it were high, steep sides where the ribbon gums grew, white and slim, among the grey-green peppermints, the treeferns and the blanket-woods.

Bel Bel stopped and looked back at Storm. Storm was standing with one forefoot raised, his ears pricked, and a puzzled expression in his eyes.

"I don't remember it," he said, "but I know I've been here before."

Then into view, between two white ribbon gum pillars, stepped Thowra, followed by his herd.

Bel Bel stood, arching her neck with pride, looking suddenly like a young mare with her first foal – so beautiful was Thowra, his feet stepping high and gracefully, his head held with such majesty as he led his herd to water.

"It is no wonder," she murmured, "that man and horse are after him." Then she and Storm went forward to greet him.

Thowra threw his head right up, his nostrils and eyes wild, as he heard their steps, but when he saw them, he whinnied joyously, and trotted towards them.

"Well, little old mother," he said, rubbing her wither, "you knew my hiding-place?" Then he exchanged nose rubs with Storm. "And you, brother of the wild wind, did you know it, or did Bel Bel bring you?"

"I brought him," Bel Bel said. "But, like you, he would

have known the way in memory: long ago Mirri and I brought you here to hide."

She walked over to greet Golden, because once she, Bel Bel, had been the one cream mare in the mountains; she had been the one that was beautiful and sought after by stallions for their herds, and by men because of her colour and her strong, sure legs which would have carried a stockman many miles over the mountains – but which never did. Now Golden was the prize, the famous and glorious mare, and Bel Bel must greet her and be proud that her son had captured – and held – her.

Thus it was that Bel Bel and Storm alone knew how Thowra vanished from his hunters, and when they heard horses – or cattle – say: "He is like wind – he must be partly a child of the wind – he comes from nowhere, he vanishes into nowhere," they would smile to themselves. Yet they, too, half-believed that Thowra had become almost magic, even though Bel Bel knew that it was she who had woven a spell over him at birth, and given him his wisdom and his cunning, all that made him seem to have the wind's mystery.

When Bel Bel and Storm at last left Thowra, at his Hidden Flat, she said something that stayed in Thowra's memory:

"Maybe," she said, "I will see you up on the Ramshead before the snows come."

As the days grew shorter, with summer turning to autumn and then to winter, he kept thinking of what she had said, and at last he set off to the face of Paddy Rush's Bogong that overlooked the range, and there he watched and watched to see if the cattle mobs had gone. When he saw no sign of man or beast, he collected his own herd and led them down, over the Crackenback and up on to the Range.

He was so glad to be back in his own particular country that he might have forgotten his feeling of foreboding about Bel Bel if he had not, very soon after climbing up above the Dead Horse Hut, seen one single hoofmark that he knew to be hers. Even so, he did not really go seeking her, feeling that if he visited all his old haunts he would surely find her. So he climbed up the Range, stepping gaily up the steep laneways of snowgrass between the tors and then climbing from rock to rock in the tors themselves, to some high rock from which he could survey miles of the lovely country. And his coat shone, in spite of getting thick for winter, and his muscles rippled beneath it.

Everything he saw, every cliff and crag, every rock or grassy glade, he knew of old, and yet he saw them now with a new intensity. He had trained himself never to forget any feature of the country through which he went, and now each tor, each weathered rock, was stamped on his memory like a photograph, and if he had to gallop through that photograph – escaping from either man or horse – he knew exactly where he could place each hard, strong hoof, exactly where he could leap, exactly where he could twist and turn.

All the world was very quiet, high up there on the Range. It was rarely that any other horses, except Storm and his herd, ever came as high, and most animals were already heading lower, anyway, before the snow came.

They saw dingoes, and occasionally a red fox, his pelt thick and good for winter, would show up against the grey-green grass. Thowra noticed how busy the scurrying insects were, from the tiny ants to the great bright blue and red mountain grasshoppers – but he, too, knew that it was going to be a heavy winter. A great deal of snow would fall to cover the bones of an old creamy mare if she chose to die up there among the high-lifted peaks of the Range.

Though the sun was shining, the first day they were up on the Range, a faint, milky haze was spreading over the sky the next morning. Already there was the winter hush of expectancy in the air.

Thowra had still not found Bel Bel, so he headed up yet higher, that second day, leading his herd through the chill dawn. The quietness was intense, there was no bird call, no rustle of leaves, and up there, not even the sound of a creek. Nothing moved except the silent-footed herd.

Into this still, quiet world, through an opening in the rocks, high above and to one side, burst Bel Bel, galloping for her life.

In a flash, Thowra knew that a man, or men, were after her and that she had taken that particular very rough way through the Ramsheads, hoping that she would not lead her hunter to himself.

Quickly, Thowra and his herd made themselves invisible among rocks, and from his hiding-place Thowra watched. He could only see one man, on a big chestnut horse, a well-bred-looking horse, and Bel Bel – Bel Bel galloping like the old mare she was, tired and not so nimble, depending on her own cunning and courage, rather than on her speed.

Then Thowra did something that no wild horse could be expected to do and which all the stockmen for ever afterwards spoke of as just another example of the mysteriousness of Thowra – he left his hidden mares and went off swiftly and silently on a line that would take him just below Bel Bel. He aimed to reach a certain clear snowgrass platform among the rocks before she did.

In the centre of this clear snowgrass, when he knew the man on his galloping chestnut would be able to see him clearly, he reared up and screamed the wild, triumphant scream of a stallion glorying in his own strength.

The man pulled up his horse on its haunches and stared at the gleaming stallion. Then, just as Thowra knew he would, he forgot Bel Bel, dug his spurs into the chestnut's flanks, and went after him at racing speed.

Thowra switched round and led him right away from Bel Bel – and away from Golden and his own mares, too.

Perhaps that stockman had recognized Bel Bel as the mother of Thowra, but he could not have hoped that Thowra would try to save her as he had, because no man would have believed – till then – that a full-grown brumby stallion would remember his mother. Quite certainly that stockman would not have expected Thowra to draw him off and *then* lead him such a terrifying gallop as could only have been devised by the most cunning of minds.

Thowra was enjoying himself. This rock and snowgrass world was his world. Not far from here was the great granite overhang under which he had been born. This was the country Bel Bel and Mirri had loved so much, the country in which he and Storm had romped as foals, and later, as irresponsible young colts.

How well he knew it all, the wild, high land, where wedge-tail eagles planed overhead, and dingoes howled to the moon at night, where a silver stallion could leap from rock to rock right to the top of a granite tor, and scream his defiance at the pursuing man.

So Thowra raced ahead of the man – and mocked him – as he had raced with Arrow and mocked him. Up and down the ribbon of lanes of snowgrass that lay between the tors, he went leaping through tumbled rocks, or up and up a tor, jumping from block to block. And Bel Bel, who had stopped to watch, saw her son, as she had once known she would, galloping free and wild, with his silver mane and tail foaming in the cold sunlight, like the spray of a gleaming waterfall. She saw him in all his perfection, poised on the top of a tor, noble cream head thrown up, as his defiant cry rang out, a great strong-shouldered, deep-chested stallion, not a fault in him, not in his powerful quarters, nor his strong, clean legs; a silver horse against the sky, free and wild, never marked by saddle, or girth, or spur, his speed never checked by a bit.

For a while she lost sight of them, but after some minutes she saw Thowra galloping along a narrow, rocky ledge below the South Ramshead, then along a ridge against the skyline, mane and tail streaming out like spun silver.

Bel Bel trotted across the mountainside. She lost sight of them again and, tired out, thought she would make towards the sandy cave where she had put her cream foal to shelter from the storm, long ago. On and on she trotted until suddenly, as she was getting near the cave, she heard the thundering of hooves. Quickly she hid herself in among some rocks. Outlined against the milky clouds was the great overhang of granite under which Thowra had been born.

As she watched, Thowra, all cream and silver strength, cleft the air above that granite rock, leapt, and landed twelve feet below, on soft snowgrass that had been his first bed, barely checked, and went galloping on.

Bel Bel saw the man on the rock's edge, trying to pull his horse back on its haunches and stop, but his speed was too great. The chestnut hurtled over, pecked badly on landing. The man somersaulted off and the horse went madly on. Stirrups flapping, reins trailing, he vanished into the trees below.

The man lay still for a while and then got slowly to his feet and started down the mountain. Bel Bel moved towards the cave, making no sound, leaving no track, and feeling supremely happy. The winter snows would come now, to cover the bones of an old mare. She had seen Thowra as she had always known he would be – a king of mountain horses.

Bearded Dragon or Jew Lizard

Chapter Twenty

THOWRA SEARCHED ALL DAY

THE WINTER SNOWS came in a wild and trememdous blizzard. Thowra knew the storm was coming and he moved his herd down to his end of the Cascades.

As he led them through the wind-moving snowgums — hearing the continual tree murmur, the word of a storm coming — he thought that this might be as heavy a winter as the one when he was a foal, and Yarraman had had to take his herd farther south. If he, Thowra, had to go south for grazing country, he would have trouble with The Brolga. Bel Bel's warning was still strong in his mind. He must not fight The Brolga till next spring, so, when he had to go lower, he took them down into the Western foothills, finding little patches of grass country.

It was an unusual winter. Snow fell deeply, in almost every storm, but on the lower levels, it was often followed by warm rain that melted the snow, and all the foothills were filled with the sound of roaring streams. Up on the Range, snow lay thick and white, drifting across the mouth of the cave, covering in a blanket the place where Thowra had been born.

Thowra had expected Golden's owner to come looking for her when the snow kept the wild horses low in the mountains, but as the rivers rose and stayed high because of frequent rain, he knew there were uncrossable barriers on every side — either rivers in flood, or deep snow. He remembered the story of the four people with long narrow boards on their feet that carried them over the snow, but these people had come so long ago... and Golden's stockman had not looked as if he could even walk far; perhaps he could only ride a horse. Untroubled, Thowra found plenty of patches of grazing country for his hungry herd over towards the stockman's track from Groggin to the Dead Horse Hut.

For months the great winds of winter blew, the rivers roared, the snow fell in silent flakes. Trees, bowed with the white blanket, sometimes snapped and broke in the night. The Black cockatoos flew crying through the mountain ash forests and up where the snowgums beat and twisted in the wind.

Once, when the snow was packed hard by the wind, Thowra left his herd and went up and up into that great world of white, where even the rocks were plastered with glittering ice patterns, and the leaves on the snowgum branches were encased in ice so that they rang together, as the wind blew, and played wild music to which a silver stallion could dance on the snow.

Golden had wanted to go with him but he had refused fiercely to take her. He knew that she was getting restless – but, after all, had not Bel Bel and Mirri always got restless and gone off from the herd before their foals were born?

All the same he did begin to worry about the way she had started to wander; for he knew she was not sufficiently bushwise to be alone – also she was too beautiful, and his greatest prize.

Thowra knew he would not be able to bear to let her be far from the herd, or far from him. He had still no understanding of how Golden was often torn between all the training and security of her former life, and the freedom of the wild life with him. Nor did he understand that, as the time for the birth of her first foal drew close, Golden began to think of her old master and his kindness of the food he had given her, and the safety of yards and well-grassed paddocks.

Gradually the long, roaring blizzards of winter, the wailing winds, and the short days, the bright frosts, and the bitter cold, changed to the swift-swinging spring storms, a hotter sun, and daylight remaining longer on the hills. The sky, on a fine day, was a deeper colour, and no longer had that glass-blue, brittle look. There was the first faint upthrust of growth on grass and shrub, the first soft, scent-laden breeze from the lower slopes. It was getting near the time for the young animals to be born. Two little dun-coloured foals arrived. Then one morning Golden had gone.

Thowra called the rest of his herd together and led them off on her tracks — amazed and pleased to find how little track she had left. She had not got the printless hooves of Bel Bel, but she had learnt her lessons in bush wisdom better than he thought.

Golden was heading for the high country, and after a while her track led them on to the stock route to Dead Horse Hut. Then Thowra saw the clear spoor of two shod horses and, in sudden, unbelieving panic, knew this spoor was a little older than Golden's. The men were ahead of her and she was following them.

He hardly stopped to wonder how the men had crossed the deep, rushing snow-waters in the river. He could not know that this year Golden's owner had left horses in a paddock on the mountain side of the river and that the men had constructed little wire bridges over which they could walk. Golden's master had got across on foot to his horses and come out to the mountains earlier than ever before.

The little foals made the herd's pace slow. At last, Thowra became so disturbed that he decided to hide his mares right off the track and go on quickly to find her.

Soon after he had left them it began to rain very hard, and in a short time all tracks were washed away — even the spoor of the shod horses. No scent lingered either. By the time that Thowra, dripping wet and muddy, was near Dead Horse Hut, he knew that Golden could have left the track in many places, and he set out to try and find her near the hut.

There was no sign of her, no sign at all, and, when he got too close to the hut, both the man's stock horse and pack-horse neighed wildly and raced in excitement. Twice, Thowra saw the man come to the door, but probably the driving rain kept him from coming farther.

Thowra searched all day, taking care not to go so close to the tame horses again, but never a track nor a sign of Golden did he find.

After midday he went back down the stock route, looking for her on either side. Just at evening, the rain stopped and a queer mixture of watery blue and pink appeared in the grey sky. The track still ran like a little creek, the bush dripped dismally and there was no trace of Golden. Thowra was feeling both worried and miserable when he went back to Dead Horse Gap.

All through the night he searched near the hut. Once he felt sure that Golden's scent came to him on the light breeze, but though he went in the direction from which it came, he found nothing. Every time he got near the yards the other horses neighed, and he knew the man came out several times to see what was upsetting them.

At last dawn broke and as the light came Thowra was standing, hidden by trees, on a little knoll not far from the hut. Suddenly he was sure he heard a faint, nickering whinny. The man came out of the hut and stood looking up the Dead Horse Ridge. Then Thowra saw a movement in the trees above the hut.

In a tiny clearing he could just make out Golden standing with a little cream foal at her feet.

The whinny sounded again – this time he was sure of it. He saw the man walk slowly and quietly towards Golden.

Then Thowra could keep silent no longer. He threw up his head and gave the great cry of a stallion to his mate.

The man hesitated once and then kept walking slowly forward, extended his hand towards the lovely cream mare. Thowra watched in bitter silence. The man drew closer and finally put his hand on Golden's neck, petting and stroking her. Golden seemed to be nuzzling him with her soft nose. Then she bent and nuzzled the foal as though showing it off, and the man bent down to it but did not touch it. Presently she nosed the foal on to its trembling legs.

As the man put his arm round her neck and started leading her towards the hut, Thowra gave another despairing cry. Golden raised her head and looked once in his direction, and then let herself be led on by her old master, the little foal wobbling beside her.

In the greatest anguish, Thowra saw her go with the man into the high-fenced yard in which she had been that first night, and heard her grateful whinnying as the man came out of the hut with a tin of food.

Thowra took one long look at the lovely mare with her foal – his foal – and went off quickly, silently back to the herd. Through the bush he went, a proud-stepping, beautiful stallion, in the prime of his life, cream and silver, dappled by light and shade as pale shafts of sunlight from the cloudy sky fell on to him through the grey-green gum leaves.

He found the herd where he had left it, the mares rather troubled at the length of time he had been away – and astounded when he told them what he had seen. But at the end of his story, Boon Boon nodded wisely and said:

"She might want to go to her old master out of care for herself and her new-born foal, but she'll want to come back in a very few days. Let us find some grazing on a sunny slope not too far from the Gap, and you can go back and see."

Thowra nodded, but all he could think of was the high fence. Aloud he said:

"She might be able to jump out again, but she'll never leave her foal."

Realizing that the man knew he was about and that he would be trying to get Golden again, Thowra understood that his usual great care to leave no trail must be doubled. But he could not bear to stay away from the hut for long in case the man tried to lead Golden and her foal straight to the lower country.

He found some better grazing for his herd, lower down, because he felt sure bad weather was coming, and facing the sun so that the grass was already getting its spring sweetness.

At dark he went back to the hut. Golden was still in the yard. He did not go up to the fence, but simply waited until morning to see if the man was making preparations for going out of the mountains.

The man only caught his stock horse, not the pack, and Thowra saw him fix a lasso to his saddle. So that was the day's plan — a hunt for the silver stallion! Thowra knew that he must now really act like a ghost horse. He moved away, leaving no trace to tell that he had ever been there.

Each night he went back, hoping Golden would show some sign of wanting to escape, but Golden only noticed her foal or, when the man appeared, showed gratitude to him for food and water. Her coat was beginning to shine; the foal was getting stronger.

Then, out of a fair and sunny afternoon, the black clouds began to roll up with speed and force. Thowra went up to the hut to see what was happening. Would the man forget he wanted to catch the silver brumby and take his mare and foal and race the storm to the lowlands?

But the storm was going to race everyone. A lashing wind was already bringing snow, when Thowra hid himself in the trees above the Gap and watched. The man came on his horse, hurrying down from the direction of Bob's Ridge where he must have been watching for him. Suddenly great swirls of snow almost blotted him from sight. The wind began to roar through the Gap, and the sound of it in the trees higher up was ugly, menacing.

Thowra shivered. This was going to be a bad storm. He saw the man stand looking in the wind direction, saw him glance back to Golden and the foal who were racing nervously round the little yard. Then the man walked over to the yard and turned Golden and the foal through the gate into the horse paddock where there was shelter.

All at once, the noise of the storm filled the air completely. It was as if nothing was left but its enormous roar, for the wild-driven snow hid the ground and the groaning trees hid all the world, blotted out everything but the immense noise.

"For the wind I have named you," Bel Bel had said, and Thowra, buffeted and torn at by the great storm, moved out of the trees and felt his way to the horse-paddock fence. Just as he reached it it seemed that he was going to be blown from his feet; he knew then that he would not possibly be able to jump the fence in this blinding storm. The wind with wild force lifted him and dashed him against a strainer, and the roar was louder still and filled with a new sound of crashing trees and branches.

Thowra felt choked with terror, but he heard Golden's scream of fear quite close and he answered her and started moving towards the sound of her cry. He went slowly, afraid to let himself be borne on the wind in case he was lifted again and thrown against a tree.

For just a moment, the snow cleared enough for him to see a tree down across the fence and the fence flat on the ground. Then the blizzard closed in again. He felt his way across the fence and was in the horse paddock.

He neighed to Golden to come, but she was there already, almost beside him, with her little foal.

"Come!" said Thowra, and with the foal sheltering between them, they went out over the fence.

Thowra led them a few yards into a little scrubby gully where they were safe from falling trees, and protected from the main force of the wind. There, the trembling little foal had a long drink, getting from its mother comfort and warmth, and relief from fear. Thowra saw that it was a filly, with mane and tail as silver as his own, neat-limbed and lovely.

"What have you named our foal?" he asked. "She should be Kunama, which means 'snow'."

"Kunama," said Golden, nuzzling the foal and then nuzzling Thowra. "Kunama." And the sweet filly wagged her furry whisk of a tail.

By then the willy-willy had passed over them and there was only the steady roar of the storm – no more trees were uprooted, and the day became lighter again. For a horse that knew the country well it was safe to move.

"Come!" said Thowra, and his word was a command.

Golden looked at her little foal and then in the direction of the storm-enfolded hut; she gave Thowra a playful nip on the shoulder and followed him up the gully and away around the back of the hut. It was wisdom to choose the safe care of her old master when a first foal was going to be born, but when Thowra's great call came through the spiralling storm, her only wish was to follow him.

Thus Thowra returned to his herd with his creamy mare and his lovely silver daughter. Thowra had won his prize for the second time, but a faint idea flitted through his head that perhaps something had to be won three times over before it was freely owned.

Kangaroo

Chapter Twenty-One

KING OF THE CASCADES

THOWRA'S FULL HERD, in that lovely spring, was becoming fairly large – large for a cream-coloured stallion who depended on speed and ghost-like movement for his safety.

Golden had Kunama, each of the three grey mares had yearlings still with them, and two had foals at foot, and there was also Arrow's black mare and her yearling. A herd of this size could not really move about without trace or track, but that hardly mattered. In the spring Thowra had only one thing to fear now, and that was Man – men could not follow a spoor as well as wild horses could, and there was no living horse that Thowra feared.

Perhaps there had never been a time when Thowra was so full of joy in being alive. The joy was different from the joy he and Storm had felt, up there on the Ramshead before they gathered their herds. This time it was a joy like owning the world, as though — and perhaps he was right — there never was and never would be again such a mountain stallion as he, Thowra.

Even the danger of Golden's master being still in the mountains and out to capture her again only seemed to add a spice to life. If there was only one man after him, why, he could lead that man a chase to end all chases! No, until the stockmen and their dogs were in the hills there was nothing really to fear, and many men and dogs could not come now, with the snow deep in the mountains above and the rivers in wild spring spate.

At the top end of the Cascades the grass was good, the sun shone, warm and life-giving. The foals grew, and the coats of all the horses became shiny.

Several times Thowra went back to Dead Horse Hut to see if anyone was there, but each time nothing moved but the wind through the Gap, swaying an old strip of green hide that hung outside the hut, rattling a piece of galvanised iron.

It was while he was up at Dead Horse Gap, one glittering spring day, that The Brolga came looking for Golden.

Boon Boon heard him first, heard his excited scream a mile away, and she gathered the herd together and started them uphill, where banks of snow still lay, all molten gold in the sunshine, to the place where Thowra would surely be coming soon. But The Brolga had already picked up Golden's spoor, and though he did not hurry, stopping to prance and snort, cavort and roar, he could easily catch a herd with young foals in it.

"You yearling colts will have to harry him," Boon Boon said to her own yearling. "But don't get too close. Draw him off, annoy him, but only a little or he may kill you."

Filled with importance, the colts trotted back to The Brolga, dancing and showing off, trying to scream like stallions – but The Brolga soon got tired of chasing these little sons of Thowra, and he went on for the herd again.

When Boon Boon saw him coming faster, she said to the other mares:

"It is better to plant the foals in the thick scrub; we can come back for them," and she led them to a patch of dense heather. Only the mares with foals went through it and planted their young ones, the others galloped around the outside; then they all joined up together again, and galloped across a flat square of snowgrass and upwards to a belt of trees. There they stopped because The Brolga was very close and they knew they might be able to dodge him in the trees.

Boon Boon was pretty sure he would not bother about any of them except Golden, whom he would try to drive back to his own herd.

"Dodge and dodge!" she said to Golden. "And don't let him drive you back."

The snowgums were tall ones and there were a few candlebarks among them with high, straight trunks. There were plenty of opportunities to dodge and move about – but, of course, that could not go on for ever. Unless help came The Brolga must win in the end – and Golden was worrying about Kunama, her lovely foal.

A fleet, light mare could swing and turn neatly round the trees; and without much effort, Golden managed to keep a thick patch of snowgums between herself and The Brolga. Twice the great grey horse tried to break through and come straight for her, but each time she had gone and was behind some other barrier – almost as much of a shining will-o'-the-wisp as Thowra himself.

The Brolga was screaming with excitement, and Thowra, way up in the snow on top of Bob's Ridge, heard him at last. When he got down, it was Golden that he saw.

Thowra gave one shattering, tremendous roar of rage, and The Brolga stopped, ears pricked, the breath snorting through his nostrils. Then Thowra came like a furious storm cloud.

"Go!" he said to Golden, and as The Brolga tried to follow her, he sprang on him with flailing hooves and bared teeth, and when he reared up, under some tall candlebarks, his great mane and tail, in the flickering, moving light and shade, did indeed look like a foaming waterfall, as Bel Bel had once thought they would.

Here was the most beautiful stallion the great mountains had ever seen, in his full strength, fighting for his mate, and it was as though everything round was hushed and still: no wind blew, and the leaves held themselves in perfect quiet. Even the sound of a little stream was muted, and neither the red lowrie nor the jays flew by. There was nothing but the pounding of hooves and tearing breath of the two huge horses.

The herd knew that it was not just for Golden that the two stallions fought, but for their lives. One must die so that the other could be the supreme ruler of the Cascade brumbies.

This time Thowra had no fear of losing.

A year ago he would have used every snowgum to help him to dodge. Now he drove his old enemy into a little open space under three tall candlebarks, and there fought him, not only with his usual weapon of nimbleness, but his new-found mature strength. The Brolga was the first horse he had ever seen fight – it was he who had eventually killed his own father.

Thowra remembered seeing him and his herd go past that cloud window on the top of the Brindle Bull, remembered the feeling of cold foreboding and fear at the sight. Now, as he fought The Brolga below the candlebarks, it seemed as if his whole life had been leading up to this moment of destroying the grey stallion. Had not Bel Bel told him to wait until he reached his full strength? Was it not the way of the wild that the old king of the stallions must be killed?

While they fought, the mares came drifting back to watch, peering through the snowgum leaves at the two powerful horses – Thowra's mares, and three of them The Brolga's daughters. The sun passed below the hills, then sunk behind the lower ranges of the Murray Valley, while the two horses strained and fought, hooves thudding on damp ground or on hide and flesh and bone. As darkness came The Brolga was beaten to the ground.

It was Boon Boon who neighed first, and then Golden – Golden who had no instinct to tell her that the old king should be killed. And Thowra, knowing his enemy would never trouble him again, left him, defeated but still living, below the shadowy trees. He had won his prize for the third time!

Thowra, half-bucking, half-kicking, shaking the foam from his glorious mane – cantered over to Golden and Boon Boon, his two favourite mares. Then he called all his herd away and they travelled down into the Cascades by the bright light of the moon. A mopoke called them, sitting white and stiff on a dead branch: possums peered at them out of the trees: a dingo went trotting past, and later they heard him howling, the answering call from his mate echoing round some wooded hollow.

The ghostly herd, all its light-coloured horses blanched by the moonlight – trotted in single file down the narrowing valley that led into the Cascades.

Thowra stepped out proudly in the lead, head and tail held high, gleaming silver. Golden followed, with Kunama's tiny head close to her flank and the little trotting feet keeping up with her swinging strides, and Boon Boon came next with the other grey mares and their foals after her, all silver-white, pale, made mysterious by the moon. Arrow's black mare, like a dark shadow, brought up the rear with the yearlings. On and on they went, at this swinging, proud walk – the king of the Cascade brumbies and his herd.

Four kangaroos stood still to see them pass, and some brown rock wallabies watched from below the moon-gleaming snowgum leaves. The slow old wombats saw the proud herd and knew a fight had been fought and won. But even the wild little bush animals knew that a horse of that unusual colour was nowhere safe. They themselves were the soft colour of the bush — able to merge into their surroundings at the first sound of an enemy, be it dingo, dog or man — but Thowra and Golden, Boon Boon's colt, and now Kunama, were only invisible in a snowstorm.

Just for a night of moonlight, just for a month of spring, while the rivers roared and the snows still lay thick, Thowra could be the proud and wonderful stallion, like no other brumby stallion ever before seen — lord of all the herds, lord of all the grey, green hills and valleys, of the shining streams, and the great rock tors. Later, when the men came once more to the mountains, he would have to gallop again with the wind, his brother, but for this short time he could live in all his wild joy and strength.

Down, down, to the Cascades, the ghost went, one after the other, and The Brolga's herd, who had come to Thowra's end of the valley, looking for their stallion, saw them coming and knew The Brolga had been beaten.

In silence Thowra came stepping downwards till he was quite close to them, then he reared up and screamed his triumph, and the valley rolled the echoes back and forth, back and forth. Thowra waited till the sound had died on the night air, and called again. This time, after the echo faded away, there was absolute quiet; no mopoke called, no dingo howled, there was not even the rustling sound of a bush animal going home — all was still. Thowra, the silver stallion, had entered his kingdom.

Even the spring, that year, was shining and perfect for a shining, perfect horse, and Thowra roamed with the big herd of brumbies up and down the valley of the Cascades, safe and unworried. But he knew two things – that he could never have a herd of that size because with them he could not escape from men; that he must find out if there was more grass country higher up the stream from his wonderful Hidden Flat so that he and Golden and Boon Boon and their foals could escape there from any manhunt.

One day, Thowra went off on his own to explore above the Hidden Flat. For hours he trotted along through the bush, watching with joy every magnificent sign of spring – a robin redbreast catching thrip on a drift of snow, a lowrie flashing red and blue across a glittering pool, the foaming streams, the new growth in the grass, buds on shrubs. Down by the Crackenback the wattles were in flower and the golden balls fell on to his back, stuck to his mane. Underfoot were the little puce Black-eyed Susan. The Bitter Pea scrub was flowering, brown and gold, nearly shoulder high to a cream stallion. The mountain world was bursting into flower, everything filled with joy in living.

Thowra crossed the river and jogged on, up on to Paddy Rush's Bogong and down the other side – careful, now, to leave no track as he neared his Hidden Flat.

Down he dropped into the valley and then started to force his way round the cliffs at the head of the grassy flats. The sun was already dropping into the west when he found a steep and dangerous way round, and moved cautiously along a wallaby track that hung perilously above the bright-glittering stream.

At last he got round the great bluff, and below him there was a narrow gorge with towering cliffs on either side. The wallaby track led on and Thowra followed it, creeping, creeping. It became wider, and though there was still the tremendous drop below, he could walk freely. The gorge ended in another bluff, but there was still a good track round it. Thowra went on. Suddenly he found himself on quite a wide rock platform looking into a wonderful valley that was big enough to graze a dozen horses for several months, and cut off all around by enormous tiers of cliffs.

This was exactly what he was looking for, if only he could find a way down. Here was a beautiful valley, and, by the way the cliffs rose, it would not be overlooked from above.

He searched all round the lookout platform, but, except for the track by which he had come, there were steep cliffs, and the platform itself jutted out into space. Thowra went back down the slope a little way, searching, searching for some track which would lead him into the valley. At one place a few turpentine bushes clung to the rocks below the track, and it seemed to Thowra that a faint path went through them. Wondering if he would hurtle into space, he braced his forefeet carefully and pushed his head through. He could still see a tiny path. He stepped gingerly forward between more bushes. The path was there all right. Forward again, and still the path went faintly through the bushes and turned down towards the bluff.

Soon the bushes ended, and Thowra was on a narrow ledge. He realized that it passed through below the lookout platform.

In half an hour he was in the valley, drinking at the stream, nibbling the grass. In the morning he would examine the cliffs for any place that he could jump down if he was ever hardpressed to escape. He wished Bel Bel was with him, but Bel Bel must have stayed on the Range for the snows to cover her.

Thowra had found a home for himself and whatever mares he wanted to bring.

Possum

Chapter Twenty-Two

BLACK MAN: SHOD HORSE

IT WAS EVENING when Thowra went home, going by way of the southern end of the Cascades. He was listening, watching – not for Man, but to find someone whom he wanted to see. However, not even a spoor had he found, no sign of horse or herd. He trotted on, enjoying the feel of the springy snowgrass underfoot, and at last he came over a little rise and saw, below him, a number of grazing horses – and among them the one he was looking for. He neighed, and his neigh was without the challenging sound of a powerful stallion, and was not the cry of a horse to its mate. The big bay stallion in the valley below heard and knew who he was and what he was saying.

Storm threw up his head and neighed in answer, then started trotting towards Thowra, while Thowra came down the slope to greet him.

"Well, brother of the wind," said Storm, "what news have you for me? I know you fought and beat The Brolga, that was good, but what else have you been doing?"

Thowra told him of Golden's recapture by her master, and of her return with him to the wild horses.

"We two are brothers of the winds and of the storms," Thowra said, "and I must indeed be brother to the wind itself, because it was the wild willy-willy that uprooted the tree over the fence and freed Golden."

Storm nodded his beautiful bay head.

"Yes," he answered, "and winds and blizzards will always befriend and protect you — it is in the bright months of summer that you are in danger."

"It is that of which I have come to speak to you," said Thowra. "Why not graze your herd near mine, here in the Cascades, and over on Paddy Rush's Bogong later? Then if Golden and Kunama and I, who the men will surely hunt, have to go, you will be there to look after the others."

Storm nipped Thowra on the wither.

"Even Mirri and Bel Bel would not have believed that we would remain brothers all our lives," he said. "Come, we will all go together until you leave us near your herd, and when the time comes for you to go over the river for summer grazing, we will go too, and I, brother, will always be near your mares and your foals."

Thus it was that Storm and his herd grazed in the Cascades almost alongside Thowra's herd, and the valley seemed almost filled with wild horses.

Fortunately, there was plenty to eat that spring. Days of

sunshine made the grass grow thick and fast, sweet and fresh – made tremendous growth on the shrubs. There would be food for all until it was time to move; and over on Paddy Rush's Bogong the grass would be untouched and afford good grazing for the summer.

The warm sun and good food made the horses sleek and shiny. The little foals romped just as Thowra and Storm had romped, four years ago. Kunama grew every day, and grew beautiful, too. Instead of Golden teaching her the wisdom of the bush, Thowra, who knew his silver daughter would have to grow up as wise as Bel Bel, taught her himself; taught her to leave no track with her tiny, neat hooves; to hide herself in tree and shrub; taught her to read the spoor of other horses; to know how old it was, how fast they were going. He showed her the tracks of the sleepy wombats and the dark wallabies, the sweet grey kangaroos – showed her where the wedge-tail eagles nest.

It was Thowra who taught her to recognize all the weather signs, just as Bel Bel had told him – how to understand the voice of the wind and the story of the clouds in the sky, how a strange, fermenting green heart to storm clouds meant wind-driven ice that could cut through a horse's hide.

He was surprised to find Kunama far easier to teach than Golden had been. Golden's mother and father had both been tame horses, living with men, and he supposed that, having been brought up by men, her instincts were not developed.

Kunama reminded him of Bel Bel, with her inborn wisdom. Perhaps, like Bel Bel, she would be given an even greater wisdom than the wisdom of mares, because she, too, being cream, would lead a hunted life, and must be wise in order to survive. Mares, Thowra knew, with foals to look after as well as themselves, often had a special understanding of the bush and weather. If, like Bel Bel and Mirri, they were "lone wolves", their wisdom, knowledge and cunning could become very great – that was why Bel Bel had been almost as much leader of the herd as Yarraman; that was why he, Thowra, having learned from Bel Bel, seemed magic to the other horses and to the men. Anyway, he knew – as soon as he saw Kunama prick her small ears, then shiver, as seven black cockatoos passed over head, flying, crying, that she would need everything he could teach her and all her own inborn wisdom, too, if she were to remain free and wild, and live her life in the mountains.

Boon Boon, who had become fast friends with Golden, took the little foal in hand sometimes, and Golden was very pleased to see her leggy filly cantering after the big grey mare.

There was one other thing in which Kunama took after Bel Bel and Thowra – she loved to wander, and this was dangerous in a foal, unless, like Thowra and Storm, it had a wandering mother. Boon Boon watched her carefully. Later, when she was weaned and could gallop faster, she would be able to go off with Thowra on his travels, but not now.

That spring the rivers were kept high for a long time, simply because there was never a great spring flood. No actual rain fell in the high mountains; there was either a snowstorm or frost and bright sunshine. The bright sun melted the snow and kept the rivers high, but if warm rain had fallen, the snow would have been washed off in a big rush and caused an enormous flood, and after that the level of the rivers would have dropped.

Thowra and Storm, when they decided to leave the Cascades, crossed their herds so near the source of the Crackenback that they did not realize how high the river really was. They were surprised when they were quite some time on Paddy Rush's Bogong before they saw the first mobs of cattle, but once they had seen the red and white beasts dotting the grassy slopes of the Ramshead Thowra, at least, became doubly watchful. Though it was a great safeguard for all the mares to have Storm near, it meant a large number of horses were very close together – and the more horses, the more difficult it was to keep them hidden.

Among the yearlings in Storm's herd was a beautiful spirited black colt with two white feet and an unusual splash of white on his flank. Thowra noticed him, and noticed his mother, too, a coal black mare. He studied her closely, thinking that she did not look like a wild horse, so he asked Storm about her.

Storm seemed worried by the question.

"The black one," he said. "Yes. I call her Lubra, but she tells me her name is Highland Lass. I'm afraid she and her yearling colt may bring trouble, too. She's an escaped tame horse. I did not steal her from the men. I took her from a dolt of a stallion, way up past the tin mine, near the headwaters of the Indi River. I only found out later that she had escaped, or maybe I would have left her alone. I thought that by the time I got her back here we would be far enough away for her owners never to follow us – now I'm not so sure."

"It's a long way," said Thowra.

"Mm! But I've since found out that she used to run in races, with a man on her back, a man wearing a bright striped coat. I think the men may value her, just like they value Golden."

"She's not bad to look at," Thowra said, "and the colt is really rather a fine young thing."

"Oh, she looks well," said Storm, "and she can go like the wind, but I've never been able to teach her any sense the way you've taught Golden. Of course, being black, she's not so difficult to hide, but as for making her take care to leave no track – it's impossible! The colt, Tambo, isn't bad at all – very intelligent in fact."

It was a lovely morning, this morning, a bright, bright dawn with pink wisps of cloud streaking the sky. Thowra left Storm and was returning to his herd when he was seized with the longing to be on his own, galloping through the cool air, up as high as he could get. So he swung round and headed off for the topmost tor on Paddy Rush's Bogong, galloping through the sharp-scented eucalyptus, galloping over silver banks of snowdaisy leaves where soon the big white flowers would star the slopes.

He leapt from rock to rock to the top of the tor and stood there in all his glorious strength and beauty, gilded by the eastern sun, silver tail and mane streaming in the breeze. He looked out over the land that was his kingdom – right out to the Main Range which he loved best of all, the Range where a horse could roam, wild and free. He wondered suddenly whether he would be allowed to let his bones bleach up there, or whether his burial place would not be chosen for him by some younger stallion, just as he had forced The Brolga out from cover to fight under the three great candlebarks. He could think of no very promising colt in the herds except Tambo. His own handsome, dun-coloured sons and the one creamy, who had grown darker as he got older, would probably wander far away.

He leapt down off the rock and started to gallop for joy, back towards his herd, when suddenly he saw a mark on the wet earth. He pulled up short on his haunches and looked again. There, straight across the damp ground, a shod horse had walked.

To his astonishment he could find no continuous track. Whoever was riding the horse was almost as cunning as himself. Without wasting time he went straight back to the herd. He found the mares very disquieted.

Boon Boon trotted over to him as she saw him coming.

"There was a man on a horse watching us," she said, "a *black* man, black as that mare, Lubra."

Golden had joined her, and Thowra saw that she was deeply troubled.

"I have heard the men talk of the cleverness of the black trackers if cattle are stolen," said Golden. "Perhaps he has come because of Lubra. I am sure she is a valuable mare. Let's go and ask her if there were any black men where she came from."

Thowra had become more troubled as Golden spoke. The very fact that the shod horse had been ridden so that he left practically no tracks, made what she had said sound like the truth. Anyway, there were all the stories that Bel Bel had told him about the aborigines. The aborigines were wild, too, and really belonged to the bush even more than the brumbies, they belonged to it like the possums did and the kangaroos.

He made the herd disperse in among the snowgums and went off himself, silently, through the trees and scrub, to find Storm and to go with him to question the black mare, Lubra.

Storm was surprised to see him again so soon.

"What is it, brother?" he asked anxiously.

"A black man on a shod horse is on the mountain," Thowra answered. "Golden suggests we should ask Lubra if there were any black trackers where she came from."

Lubra, with Tambo, was by a pool in a little stream when they found her.

"A black man," she said, looking fearful. "Yes, there was. He was clever at finding any beasts that had wandered. I think he will be looking for me."

"She's a foolish mare," said Storm, as they went off, "but I think she knows there was a black man all right."

"I had better take a good look around late this evening," Thowra muttered. He was troubled. It was not only Golden it seemed who was going to bring danger to them.

All day the brumbies remained under cover of the trees. Thowra felt a little better by the end of the day because all the bush animals and birds behaved quite normally – which they would not have done if there had been men about. He saw a dingo go slowly along a track as though he had no thought in the world except his next meal. Even the jays gave no warning sounds, only chattered at a poor, inoffensive porcupine. Then just before sunset, Storm appeared.

"I have seen the black man," he said, "and *he* has seen Lubra. He appeared just like a shadow between the trees — his horse dark brown, his own clothes grey, or green, or dirty, so that they did not show up."

"You look after the herds," Thowra suggested, very worried, "and I'll go off now and see if there are any other men about."

The bush was quite quiet as he went on his scouting expedition. The only sounds were the normal rustlings and movements of evening, as the wombats came out to sun themselves in the last pleasant rays, as the animals who fed by day went off to their homes, and those that fed by night started to stir. No possums would come, he knew, till that strange moment that belongs to no time at all, when it is neither dark nor light. Then their pointed faces, that are both curious and wistful, would peer down on him from the gumtrees, and he would smell the distinctive possum smell, more pungent than eucalyptus, but very like it.

Though Thowra searched and searched through the country that he knew so well, he could find no sign of the black stockman, or of anyone else. All was quiet. Down by the Crackenback crossing the river moved, black and silver in the starlight, the sand unmarked by anything except the bush animals and the receding flood levels. A tawny owl hooted softly. It seemed that all the bush was at peace except he,

Thowra, with the unquiet mind and the skin that prickled.

He went back to the herd, still feeling that somewhere in that peaceful bush there had been eyes watching him.

The next day everything was absolutely quiet and the bush creatures moved about just as usual. Thowra wandered around several times, and again at dusk and during the early part of the evening. He saw nothing strange, heard nothing strange, and this time he felt nothing strange. He was less worried by the time he got back to the herd.

The night was very calm, very still. The Southern Cross hung, bright and clear, above all the country around the headwaters of the Indi. It was not possible even to imagine any lurking danger in the friendly bush.

Thowra and Golden went to drink together from a moss-fringed pool at the head of a long glade. The water in this particular pool was very good and they were drinking it slowly, relishing its flavour, sucking it through their teeth, letting it lap gently into their nostrils. A puff of wind came from the south. Thowra lifted his head. All at once he became tense. There was a sound borne on the wind, a sound he had never heard before – as if wood was knocking against wood, but he could not guess what it was. Following the sound, the wind carried a scent to them. Thowra sniffed and listened, listened and sniffed.

"It is the scent of Man," he whispered. "They are close, and I don't know what they are doing."

Chapter Twenty-Three

The Leap from the Cliff

THOWRA AND GOLDEN moved silently back to the trees where Kunama was sleeping. Boon Boon was nearby, her head up, smelling the air, ears pricked forward.

"It's time that Golden and Kunama should hide," Thowra said. "You come, too, Boon Boon, and I will show you the track in and out of my secret valley. We must hurry, and I will send your colt to tell Storm we are gone, and that I will come back when you and the foal are safely hidden."

Golden stirred the little filly and they all four set off in the night, walking silently at first till they were well away from the men, then trotting, trotting, keeping to the snow-grass lanes where they would leave no track. In the starlight each creamy was just a hint of a pale horse moving: Boon Boon was invisible.

They had quite a long way to go, and would have to

hurry. Over the top of the mountain and down, along and along on a gently dropping grade, silent-footed over the dead leaves of peppermint forest, they went; sometimes using the rocks of an old watercourse as a road on which they could leave no hoofmark. They trotted, trotted, on, and on, and on.

Suddenly alongside there hopped three silver-grey kangaroos.

"Hullo!" Thowra said, startled. "Why do you travel at night, and where do you come from?"

"Why, O Silver Horse, we come from the other side of the Crackenback, and we travel at night because there is going to be trouble on the mountains."

"Trouble with Man?" asked Thowra.

"Yes. In all the lore of the kangaroos – all the tales that pass from kangaroo to kangaroo throughout the country – it is told that when the white men get the black men to help them catch animals, their traps are made with the cunning of both black and white."

"Traps!" said Thowra, thinking of the sound of wood striking wood.

"We, O Silver Horse, were camped near the Crackenback when you came down last night. We saw you, but we don't know if the men who slept there did."

Thowra felt his coat pricking again. After all, eyes had watched him.

"No one moved," the biggest kangaroo went on. "They watched for a long time, waiting in case you came, because the black man had not seen you, and they wondered where you were — but they must have gone to sleep by the time you came down to the water, because no one moved."

"You heard them talking, then?" Thowra said. "I never smelt or heard their horses."

"Their horses were left in a hollow a mile away. Yes, we heard them talking. The man who owned your mare, here," he nodded towards Golden, "wants her back, and when he and his friends met the black tracker who had come looking for a big black mare, they all got together, planning a big brumby drive into the yard they have made. But they won't get you!" he looked knowingly at Golden. "Well, so long, we must be going."

The three kangaroos hopped on their way.

"Come on," said Thowra. "There's no time to lose."

On, through the night they went, cantering, now, wherever possible, and the smell of the peppermints was sweet and strong. At last they reached the Hidden Flat and dropped down into it, then Thowra told them to follow him closely while he led them round into his Secret Valley.

It was a perilous journey in the dark. When Kunama heard a stone start down, knocking against other stones, and then bouncing from rock to rock, down, down, till the sound of its falling was lost in the darkness and the depth, she started back in fear, but Thowra said, "Come!" and Golden said "Come!", and Boon, behind her, said "Go!"

Down they went, following Thowra, their rockhard hooves clinging like goats' feet. At last they were at the bottom, standing by the starlit river, with the looming cliffs above them, and only the memory of their breathless descent.

"I must go back to the others and warn them," Thowra said at last. "Hide here. When daylight comes you will see plenty of grass. I should be back here by tonight."

He turned to go, the pale shape of him showing against the cliff, then swung back again, starlight reflecting in his eyes. "If I get caught," he said, "I will free myself, somehow, and return to you."

Then up the cliff he went, leaving the two mares and the filly foal behind in the strange Secret Valley.

This time Thowra really hurried. He thought of his mares and of Storm, and the sound he had heard of a trap yard being built. Probably the men would wait till midday or afternoon to start their brumby drive. They would know that the horses went out feeding in the cool early morning, and would be harder to find. At the back of his mind, like a dream, was the faint memory of galloping, galloping beside his mother, one oppressive afternoon, when the men had built a trap yard and were driving all the wild horses through the bush.

On, on he went. Dawn came slowly – silver-coloured and fresh. A little grey thrush burst into song right beside a stream where he stopped to drink. Thowra, sweating and breathless, hurried on.

As he drew near to the top of the mountain he moved with even greater caution, but there was nothing to suggest danger, nothing to suggest the cordon of stockmen and dogs that was already waiting at the foot of the mountain, ready to close on the horses and drive them towards the trap yard.

He hastened first to find Storm, and had he not known

his brother of the winds and the blizzards so well, he might have missed him, but as he looked along a band of snowgums, he seemed to see among the leaves and the boughs the shape of a noble horse.

Storm looked in amazement at the sweating Thowra.

"What has happened?" he asked.

Thowra told him what he knew, and added:

"All the horses must try and get through as best they can, and in ones and twos they have more chance."

Storm nodded.

"It's no good going south, though. That's where Lubra and the black tracker came from."

"That's true," Thowra agreed. "Better to go, for a while, into all that wild tangle of valleys off the Crackenback, where I hid with my first small herd. And I've just come up that way and seen no one."

"Lubra is a foolish one," said Storm, obviously wondering what trouble she might bring. "Well, we must go."

Thowra stretched his creamy nose forward and nipped him on the neck.

"I hope we two meet again after today, brother," he said.

The two stallions went off through the bush, each to warn their mares – the superb silver horse, and the noble bay with the strong head and the great, kindly eyes.

"Go!" they said to each mare with her foal at foot. "Go!" they said to the yearling. "Don't keep together – a foal with its mother, yes, but otherwise each one has a better chance alone."

And soon there were flitting shadows moving through

the bush, hiding here, hiding there, but all travelling north-eastwards – mares with little foals, sometimes two dry mares together, colts, fillies, and, alone but watchful, the bay stallion and the silver one.

The first thing that made Thowra realize they were too late and that the men were closing in already was when he noticed two wallabies hastening nervously towards him, and then a dingo close behind.

"Man!" the dingo snapped, and went hurrying on.

Thowra knew it was too late, but seeing his other two grey mares he joined them, and led them to a deep creek bed he knew, and told them to make their way silently along it until they thought the men had gone, and then at nightfall, if all was well, to aim for the Hidden Flat.

Just then a blue heeler cattle dog came trotting up the creek.

Thowra leapt up one of the rocky sides.

"Keep going," he neighed to the mares. "The dog will follow me."

The dog did follow him, but in the long years since the first brumby drive Thowra had learnt how to deal with one dog, and he waited and kicked out at him. The dog knew better than to let himself be hurt, so he kept his distance, and barked.

Thowra went at him with teeth bared and ready to strike. As the dog leapt to one side, Thowra was after it. But the dog's master had heard the scuffle and was rushing towards them, cracking his whip so that other men and other dogs would come to his assistance.

The Leap from the Cliff

Suddenly, all was wild movement below the great mountain ash trees. There were men, horses, dogs. Whips were cracking, voices shouting – and Thowra had to turn and head up the mountain again, as almost every other horse in the two herds would shortly have to do. For men were everywhere on the mountain – men from the Murray, after Golden, men from Benambra after Lubra, men from all the Snowy River country who had come to join in the hunt. There were men, too, who were among the very best riders of the mountain land. There were men on blood horses, men on nippy stock horses, men with splendid dogs. And they were all after Golden and Highland Lass whom Storm had named Lubra.

Thowra thought it was worth trying to drop quietly into the top of the deep creek bed and hide himself until the chase had gone by. There was a thicket of snowgum and hop scrub ahead, leading right to the edge of it. He dived into the scrub, pushing through it quickly, and down a rocky crag to the creek. He stopped among the scrub and rocks at the bottom, trying to breathe without sound.

There was no escaping! Two dogs came barking madly after him. Thowra stood his ground and struck at them, but again there came the sound of a whip. With a parting slash at the dogs, he leapt out and up the creek. A rope whistled and fell short; the man was quite close. Quick as a thrown knife, Thowra wheeled round in an attempt to get away downstream, while the man coiled his lasso again. The dogs closed in. He bit one and kicked the other – then saw another man and his horse standing in the creek below him.

He bounded up a rock rib. There, at the top, was a third man coming towards him.

Thowra went galloping on through the bush – the great creamy horse with his mane and tail foaming out behind, galloping, galloping, and being edged upwards by the men all the time. Now that his freedom might again be lost, he felt more tremendously alive than ever before. He was aware of every cream hair in his coat, as though each one was tingling, feeling, listening. He was aware of his ears pressed back, his nose, his keen eyes. He was aware of the hardness of his hooves, of the immense strength in the muscles of his legs, his quarter, his shoulders. He was aware of all these things, and of himself as one great, powerful, silver stallion leaping up and up the mountain, harried by dogs and by men.

"O strength, and power, and all Bel Bel's cunning, don't fail now," Thowra thought: and once again Bel Bel's voice seemed to echo through the bush, ringing in his ears above the sound of hooves. "*For the wind I have named you…*"

"Swiftly, swiftly," he thought, and all the time the noise of the drumming hooves grew louder, coming from all around, echoing off the rocks, sounding through the snowgums. There were horses galloping up the mountain from every direction, all the wild horses being driven by many mounted men and their dogs. Soon they would be driven along the grazing grounds. In a sudden flash, Thowra thought of the direction from which the sound of the men building their trap yard had come. Yes! they were being driven towards it.

He shot into some thick snowgums, and the touch of the

leathery leaves on his hide made him feel the size and strength of himself afresh. There was still one possible line of escape – the craggy ravine in which he and Storm, as foals, had hidden from Arrow. He felt sure the trap yard was just close to it.

A man on a fine black horse was coming up close to him now. He heard the whistle of a rope, and desperately propped and swung away. The rope clipped him on the ear and fell to the ground like a dead snake. The pounding of hooves was greater than ever. Now six horses were running with him, galloping, sweating, straining, blowing, their flanks touching his flanks, their hot breath mingling with his. He could see the wildness of their eyes. The mare he had taken from Arrow's herd was there – and the foolish mare, Lubra, with Tambo alongside. He wished he could see Storm.

Now they were at the grazing ground and another mob of horses was galloping to join them. The noise of hoof-beats was like the roll of thunder – and as terrifying. Thowra could feel the terror running through the mob.

More horses joined them all the time. Storm must be somewhere, but there were too many, all bunched together, madly galloping, for Thowra to see him.

Suddenly he noticed – with eyes trained to pick out anything unusual – a long fence hidden in trees and bushes. The mob were racing alongside it already. It must be the wing of a yard, like the wings on the yards the men built for their cattle. The horses were, even now, as good as caught. Thowra strained his eyes to see the yard. He guessed it must be hidden by a patch of scrub ahead. The only way of escape was for the whole mob to break when they reached the scrub.

"Swing west! Swing west!" he urged. "Tell every horse, swing west!"

All the men who were not behind the mob of horses were riding that western flank, shouting and cracking their whips. It would be difficult to break through them.

"Come on! Come on!" Thowra called. "Swing west and break through them!" And he swung himself, forcing the others on his flank to swing with him, and led them off at a tremendous pace. The others followed.

The men from the rear immediately galloped towards the flank, trying to head them, and those out on the wing already redoubled their shouts and whip cracking.

Thowra galloped towards them as he had never galloped before, and heard the mob pounding along with him. But the men were racing across, and there were so many men that there seemed to be no space between them.

Thowra suddenly screamed to the mob, and charged one man on a lightweight liver chestnut, knocking him flying. Just then he got a blinding cut across the eyes with a whip, and even if he had succeeded in passing one man, it looked as though there were twenty more closing in on him. He charged again with utter desperation – aware of the hesitation in the mob behind him – but the whips cracked and then two ropes came flying, and he knew that the men wanted him more than any of the other brumbies except Lubra, now that Golden was not there. He turned before another rope could entangle him, and found the mob had turned already.

The Leap from the Cliff

Despair seized him for a moment, but then hope followed. He was now running straight towards the long fence instead of beside it – and could, therefore, jump it. The ravine was on the other side... there was still a chance.

Once more he was almost in the lead, though he was careful not to get right out in front, careful to see that his cream hide was partly hidden by the madly fleeing bays, browns, blacks, and chestnuts. The smell of fear rose all round him. He must keep calm. There was the fence looming ahead. The leading horses had seen it and were trying to slacken speed, and there were men trying to swing them away from it, lest they all crashed through it and into the deep ravine.

Thowra keyed himself to jump, hoping that no horse would dash into him as he took off. He shortened stride, gathered himself together, and sprang with all his great strength. Up, up, forelegs bent close to his body, up, up, he went.

"Higher, higher!" he told himself, for it was a very high fence.

He heard a shout ringing out above the thunder of hooves and the general shouting and whip cracking. The men had seen him, but he knew he was clearing the fence. He was away, even though he could see that the landing was rough and bad on the other side.

He landed neatly and safely, and in two paces was at the edge of the ravine. He knew exactly where he was and how to get down. As he jumped over the edge he heard a crash. The brumbies had dashed into the fence and broken it.

How much they had broken of it he did not know because no horses came into the ravine while he was there, and while he hastened away to safety he neither saw nor heard the men trying to force the brumbies away from the lip of the cliff, and round up those who had quickly broken through again.

Thowra went down the ravine a long way, even though it led in the opposite direction from the Secret Valley, until he came to another deep cleft that ran into it from the eastern side. He turned up this, often looking behind to see if he were being followed. When he had gone right up this one to its head, he took off cautiously through the bush. Though he could see no one and heard no unusual sound, he was convinced that he was being followed. He felt that prickling in the coat... Unless he was sure he was safe he did not like to go straight towards the Secret Valley.

An hour passed, and there was still no sign of man. He turned slightly in the direction of the two valleys. Soon it would be evening, but he could not rid himself of the feeling of being watched.

He stood still in a clump of peppermint and blanket-wood and waited. After a while he saw, coming quietly, so quietly through the trees and heading for the Hidden Flat, Storm and Tambo!

With a great gladness he greeted Storm, but there was no time to hear anything about the rest of the herd, because Storm said:

"I hoped we'd find you. Lubra is caught, and Golden's master saw you escaping and has got the black tracker with him to try and find you. Best to go for your Secret Valley, leaving no tracks. Tambo and I will go much lower down the stream and work our way up into the Hidden Flat. Farewell, brother."

"Farewell," said Thowra, going off alone, swiftly through the bush.

He could not help wondering if this was the last time he would glide like a shadow through the tall trees, and for a moment he felt as if he were another horse, seeing himself in all his silver magnificence.

He had gone about five miles when he heard a sound. Someone was close! Then he saw them – Golden's master, the black tracker, and the man on the fine black horse, and with them four dogs.

Thowra stood perfectly still, melting into the scrub, but a dog whined and set him, and he knew he must fly like the wind.

He was determined he would not lead them towards the Secret Valley, but there was no choice really, for that was the way they drove him.

The men were well mounted, but Thowra had no weight at his back and he could go faster. If only he could lead them on till evening... Men could not see in the dark... He kept on trying to dodge and twist, to turn them away from the route to his two valleys, but it was all that he could do to keep ahead of them.

As he galloped, he knew suddenly that he could not bear to let them catch him – he would rather be killed trying to get away. If they drove him on and on towards the

Secret Valley he might or might not reach the cliffs. But if the men were close behind he would jump, anyway, not waiting to find his safe way down.

Thowra had barely a chance to look back but he was sure one horse went lame, the big black, and that there were now only two following him.

The light was fading, fading. Soon it would be the possum light, the timeless area between night and day – the light that might be Thowra's light, too. A wind came from the north, quite suddenly, *his* wind, and there was the smell of rain. The tiredness from the day's galloping dropped away from Thowra; he felt renewed. This was his hour as well as the possums'. The light was almost gone and there was rain coming to cover tracks. He galloped and galloped and was well-enough ahead to choose his own line over the cliffs.

There were the two candlebarks that marked the place to jump. Thowra gathered himself together, keen-eyed in the darkness. The wind enfolded him. Came the edge of the cliff and he leapt – on to the grassy platform he had tried as a landing place before, felt it firm beneath him as he landed, and took off again instantly for the next leap. And all that the men saw was the pale ghost of a horse hurtling through space and wind, and when they reached the edge, there was nothing to be seen at all; just the sound of a stone falling a long way off.

Even the black tracker saw no way a horse could have got down alive, nor did he imagine that there might be a beautiful valley below, where Golden and Kunama and Boon Boon were hidden. The men turned back through the darkness, saddened by the thought that they had chased a beautiful horse over such a cliff. In the night, there came rain to wash away all signs of tracks, and in the morning the black man took Lubra and left for the south.

Golden's master looked for her all through that summer, and even in the summers that followed, but not a sign of her did he see. And though, time and again, he told how the silver stallion had hurtled over the cliff, there grew up around the campfires stories of a great silver stallion seen galloping over wind-packed snow way up on the Ramshead Range; of a ghost horse that drank at the Crackenback River; of a horse that all men thought was dead appearing in a blizzard at Dead Horse Hut and vanishing again; of the wild stallion cry that could only be Thowra's. But no man knew where the son of Bel Bel roamed.

GLOSSARY

BLACK SALLEE TREES. Eucalyptus with dark green and black trunks, narrow, dark leaves. They grow thickly in damp places and are often hung with a grey-green fungus called Old Man's Beard.

BLANKET-WOODS. Tall shrubs with a woolly leaf. Mostly grow around creeks.

CANDLEBARKS. Tall, beautiful eucalyptus trees, with cream or white bark that is splashed with red in summer time.

CHRISTMAS BUSH. There are a lot of native shrubs called by bushmen *Christmas Bush* because they flower at Christmas time. This one has a white flower with some mauve spots inside it.

FLYING PHALLANGER. A possum that glides from tree to tree or from a tall tree to the ground.

GANG-GANG. A dark, grey-green mountain cockatoo. The male has a scarlet crest. They are very fond of the gum-nuts (the fruit of the gum trees, containing seed). They come down to the valleys in bad weather.

KILLING GALLOWS. Looks rather like a windmill and is used for raising the bullock when killed for beef.

KURRAWONG. Big black birds with a little white on them – sometimes they are grey. They are known as the mountain magpies, and have a clear, bell-like call as well as a harsher one. They are in our garden all winter.

LOWRIE. A parrot of royal blue and scarlet, very bright.

Glossary

LYREBIRD. A dark-brown bird which lives in the damp, thick bush around creeks. It has a magnificent tail which it spreads in the shape of a lyre. It can mimic any sound.

MOPOKE. A little grey-white night bird of the owl family. His cry at night – "Mopoke" – can often be heard.

SKILLION ROOF. A roof built out from the main building, making a sort of lean-to shed.

SNOWGRASS. Grey-green, springy, tussocky grass which grows in the snow country. Lovely grass on which to run.

SNOWGUM. Also called a White Sallee. It is a eucalyptus that usually grows in the mountains, quite high up, and sometimes is twisted to very strange shapes. Its bark is frequently marked like a jig-saw puzzle in green, grey, white, red, pink, yellow, and orange.

TEA-TREE. Many different sorts of shrubs and trees, generally with a papery bark and a small white flower. Usually grow near creeks. They have a leaf rather like a tea leaf.

WHITE RIBBON GUMS. These are the eucalyptus trees that the native bear eats, known as ribbon gum or manna gum. In the mountains they grow very tall with white trunks, perfectly straight, like marvellous pillars.

WILLY-WILLY. Wind that goes round and round and upwards, and can bluster along at a tremendous pace, whirling everything round and up. When really fierce it is a tornado and uproots trees in a few seconds.

Postscript

We live in a fairly isolated area in the foothills of the Snowy Mountains in Australia, where we have lived since the 1930s. My house is high up on Towong Hill, and looks down on to a river flat which leads to the Murray River, on the eastern border of our property. If I look towards the mountains, I can see the highest peak in Australia, Mount Kosciusko, and in the winter, as their name suggests, the mountains are covered with snow. We have real-life ponies outside, dogs, sheep, cattle and ducks, as well as wildlife like kangaroos, wombats, black cockatoos, gang-gang parrots and lowries.

Because we were living so far away from anywhere, my children had most of their primary schooling by correspondence, and packets of school work came by mail. They found the stories that came for them to read were rather dull, so I decided I must write one myself (I had already had six adult books published). I was missing the mountains terribly, because I was pregnant at the time and unable to ski or even ride very far because my children were so young. This, together with the memories of travelling with my husband before we settled in Towong Hill, skiing and climbing mountains in South America, North America and New Zealand, meant the story had to be about mountains. And of course, for the children, it had to be about horses. Hence *The Silver Brumby* – the wild mountain horse.

Then each child wanted a book and so the series proceeded – with *Winged Skis* (about skiing, naturally) for the boys who did not really like horses. Other children wrote to me asking for more and more Brumby stories, so they went on.

When the film of *The Silver Brumby* was made in 1993, I was closely involved and consulted during the scripting and some of the shooting. Caroline Goodall, who played me in the film, has since become a very good friend.

Horses have been part of my life since childhood. My father was General Sir Harry Chauvel, Commander of the Desert Mounted Corps, two regiments of which made the last mounted cavalry charge in the history of war – the charge of Bethsheba in Palestine in 1917. There are still some hundreds of wild brumbies in the Snowy Mountains, and their numbers are growing. Animal liberation groups are against any culling of these wild horses. Tragically, this could mean the eventual deterioration of the breed.

ELYNE MITCHELL